Unexpected Reunion
Carolyn Greene

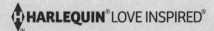

Recycling programs for this product may not exist in your area.

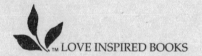 ™ LOVE INSPIRED BOOKS

ISBN-13: 978-0-373-87894-9

UNEXPECTED REUNION

www.Harlequin.com

Printed in U.S.A.

We went through fire and water,
but you brought us to a place of abundance.
—*Psalms* 66:12

Why have I found such favor in your eyes…?
—*Ruth* 2:10

This book is dedicated to the memory of
my dear friend and fellow author Charlotte Lobb
(a.k.a. Charlotte Carter), who loved, challenged, and
treasured all those who were fortunate enough to
know her, whether in person or through her stories.

Acknowledgments

To Day Leclaire, with gratitude and affection,
for 23 years of friendship, brainstorming,
learning, and laughter.

And much appreciation to Yuko Kimura-Koenig
for checking my use of Japanese words.
Any mistakes are all mine.

And thanks to my editor, Melissa Endlich,
for loving my idea for the Southern Blessings series
and welcoming me into the Love Inspired fold.

Chapter One

It wouldn't have been so hard to go through boxes of the elderly Bristows' belongings if they hadn't included the Japanese kissing dolls that used to sit on top of the piano where their grandson Gray Bristow had taught her to plunk out "Chopsticks."

Ruthie Chandler touched the small porcelain faces together so the two pairs of puckered lips met once again. The boy doll's premolded hair still showed evidence of having been darkened with a black marker to look like Gray. The girl doll's locks carried the remnants of a red marker and her face sported brown hand-drawn freckles like Ruthie's. Some gentle cleaning should easily remove the marks—if not the memories—from the smooth white finish. She expected the charming, nostalgic set to sell quickly and move on to a new home where it would foster new memories.

Ruthie set the pieces aside and wished it was as easy to set aside the bittersweet memories they stirred in her.

In the adjoining shop, Savannah must have noticed something on her face or in her demeanor. The pretty blonde moved past the wedding dress on display and joined her, where she peered over her shoulder at the pair of dolls in her hand. She didn't say anything at first. Didn't need to.

Her friend had been with her at Wednesday night Bible study the evening she'd received the Dear Jane letter from Gray four years ago, so Savannah must have recognized the shell-shocked expression that apparently had crept back onto her face. Ruthie mindlessly rubbed her thumb against her left ring finger where the white-gold engagement ring used to sit. Back then her world had been filled with hope for a future with the man who'd been the Boaz to her Ruth.

A sentimental romantic, Ruthie had loved the part of scripture where the biblical Ruth asked the kindly Boaz, "Why have I found such favor in your eyes…?" and the happy ending where the couple blessed her mother-in-law, Naomi, with a grandson named Obed. She had imagined the baby she and Gray might have someday—a child with her then-fiancé's dark hair and almond-shaped eyes, which hinted at his grandmother Naoko's Japanese heritage. A child he would protect. A child she would teach to savor the memories of its growing-up years. A child they would raise in the church and who would love God.

Unfortunately, her then-fiancé's emails from Afghanistan had become short and to the point…which she had told herself was for reasons of military security. But that hadn't explained their platonic tone. The messages she'd received during the three months prior to the breakup could have been written to his sister. Something had happened just before that Thanksgiving…something Gray had alluded to but couldn't, or wouldn't, tell her.

Savannah had offered to make her wedding dress, one she claimed would be as beautiful as the bride. It would have been beautiful, no doubt. But it hadn't come to pass.

Her friend's compliment had made her blush at the time. Not by a long stretch would she call herself beautiful. Not with her fine red hair, freckles and lanky figure. Back then, she had begun to wonder, however, if Gray had become disenchanted with the image in the photo she'd sent him. Now she just tried not to think about it.

"The Bristows must have been busy with their spring cleaning," Savannah said, and gestured toward the stack of boxes. "You'll have plenty of nice things to sell at the sidewalk sale. Hopefully, the weather will be warmer than today." The pretty blonde's limp always seemed worse during cool weather.

This portion of the historic Carytown district in Richmond, Virginia, was often referred to as the "Mile of Style." Tucked away in the 1930s-era Cary Court Park & Shop, like a quiet cove in a bustling harbor, a cluster of tiny businesses gathered under the name Abundance. Inside, three stores—Ruthie's Gleanings, Savannah's Connecting Threads and Milk & Honey, a café run by Paisley, another former college roommate—shared the same roof and exterior walls and were separated only by decorative waist-high room dividers that encouraged browsers to wander from one shop to the next. Although business was slow this Tuesday afternoon in late April, the upcoming annual sidewalk sale would draw shoppers from all over Virginia with its upscale trendy and vintage offerings.

Ruthie shook away the nostalgic cobwebs that clung

to the corners of her heart and turned her attention back to the Bristows. "Ever since Pop brought Sobo home and put her in the hospital bed in their spare room, she's been directing him on clearing out the clutter in there. I wish she would just rest and focus on healing."

After Ruthie's mother had died suddenly in a work-related accident eleven years ago and she'd had no place to go, Naoko Bristow had taken her in and gained legal guardianship for her final two years of high school. But they hadn't stopped there. Though she'd known them only from church, they had treated her as if she were their own flesh-and-blood granddaughter, insisting she call them by their grandparent names: Sobo, the Japanese word for grandmother, and Pop, a Southern endearment for grandfather. The elderly pair had even sent her off to college and set her up in their Fan District rental house with two roommates. An added bonus to gaining these adoring grandparents had been meeting and falling in love with their grandson.

The couple had been there with her at church the night she'd learned Gray didn't want her anymore. They had handed her the letter, in fact. And on hearing the message inside the Afghanistan-postmarked envelope, they'd grieved right along with her...grieved as much for his broken faith as for the broken engagement.

"Right," Savannah said. "Tell that to the tiny dynamo who forgot she's in her seventies and climbed a trellis to prune roses."

If it weren't for the broken hip that had resulted from the fall, Ruthie would have applauded Naoko's youthful energy. Instead, the incident served as a reminder that time eventually catches up to even the most active of people.

"The doctor said her body also thinks it's younger than it is, so her recovery time should be quick."

"Thank God for that." Savannah picked up the girl doll, stared at the red hair and freckles and gazed back at Ruthie. "You're going to keep these, aren't you?"

"And torture myself? I don't think so." Every time she saw them, she would no doubt remember Gray's large, warm hands covering hers while he guided her fingers over the piano keyboard. Remember the way he had peeked at her when he thought she wasn't watching…but she was always watching, and they'd both shyly look away. She'd remember the way her heart went rat-a-tat-tat at his nearness on the mahogany bench. Between sneaking glances at Gray, her gaze had often drifted to the tiny porcelain dolls he had jokingly—or not so jokingly—customized to look like them, and which had prompted the human counterparts to steal kisses when Pop and Sobo weren't looking.

Outside, a sudden movement broke her reverie. A dark silver-gray sedan that looked like the civilian version of a police car spun into the lot and double-parked in front of Abundance. The car door swung open, and a black-haired man emerged from the driver's side.

Savannah's eyes widened in surprise. "Speaking of torture, it looks like you have a visitor. Gray Bristow, if I'm not mistaken." She sidled closer to Ruthie as if to shield her. He would never hurt her physically, but Savannah had been with her at the Wednesday night Bible study when Ruthie received his letter and knew the heartbreak he had caused her. "Do you want me to stay?"

"No, I can handle it." Maybe. Somehow. *Dear God,*

please give me the strength to handle the obstacles that cross my path.

Her friend eased back to her own shop, casting wary glances over her shoulder while Ruthie struggled to gather her wits enough to face the man who still sneaked into her dreams at night.

Almost guiltily, Ruthie stuffed the kissing dolls back into one of the boxes she hadn't finished unpacking. Pretending to busy herself with polishing an antique beveled-glass jewelry casket, she watched him yank open the door and blink off the effects of the bright sun as he stepped inside.

The first thing she'd always noticed about Gray, physically, was his erect military bearing. He moved like a man on a mission. Three and a half of the four years after she'd received his breakup letter, the army had either kept him overseas or sent him to a distant stateside assignment. The past six months since his return to Richmond and civilian life, she had carefully choreographed her visits to his grandparents to avoid encountering Gray. She suspected he had done the same.

He had changed a lot since she'd last seen him. The casual blue T-shirt strained at biceps strengthened during his time in the army, and he actually seemed a little taller, which could have been merely an illusion from his don't-mess-with-me attitude. But the biggest change she noticed was in his face. Pain—and maybe fear?—lurked in his handsome features.

He took off his sunglasses and pushed a hand through his wind-ruffled hair. When his gaze landed on Ruthie, she caught a flash of an expression she couldn't identify before his handsome features turned grim. He walked toward her, his movements effortless and silent.

Ruthie turned to face him. She wished that they could erase what had gone wrong between them and start over. She wanted him to believe again. In the God he'd begun to doubt while in Afghanistan. And in a future together with her.

But that wasn't going to happen. Certainly not judging by the look on his face. If his expression showed her so bluntly "it's not going to happen," then what might hers be revealing to him? She'd always been told her emotions were like clear glass…anyone could read right through them, and she prayed a futile prayer that he would not see how much she'd missed him. How much she still hurt from his rejection.

What a fool she was to ever believe that she'd gotten over him. She lifted her chin. The smart thing to do would be to simply stand there and treat him like an ordinary customer, but everything in her being urged her to beg him to take her back…on any terms.

"It's Sobo," he said, ignoring the formality of a hello and getting straight to the point. His voice sounded strained, as if he had run the entire way here. "She's been taken to the emergency room, and it's serious."

Ruthie caught fear rippling in his coffee-brown eyes, and her heart went out to him, while her mind flashed through a thousand possibilities. "Did she hurt herself again?" she asked. "How did she get out of bed?"

"I'm not sure of all the details," he said. "I called Pop from work to check on him and Sobo, and the rescue squad was already loading her into the ambulance. I've already spread the word to the rest of the family." He shifted where he stood, the nervous action revealing his unspoken desire to go to his grandparents and stand by them during this difficult time. "There's a blood clot in her leg. A complication from the hip fracture. The danger is that it could break loose and travel to her lung." He reached for her hand to urge her along. "Come on, I'll drive you to the hospital. Pop shouldn't be alone in the waiting room. He needs us."

Ruthie started toward the door with him, then turned back to get her purse from behind the counter. She reached to move a room divider to close off the shop to customers, but a moment of panicked indecision swept over her. Her gaze landed on an eavesdropping Savannah.

"Go!" said Savannah with a sweeping motion of her hands. "Paisley and I will take care of your customers."

Relieved, Ruthie thanked her and raced out the door with Gray.

He'd hoped—since he no longer prayed—that he wouldn't feel a thing for Ruthie when they met again. Stupid of him to think it for even one short minute. Everything he'd ever felt for her came rushing back the instant he caught sight of those big greenish-brown eyes and those wild freckles. Twenty-nine. There were twenty-nine freckles, and he'd taken delight in counting each and every one, before he'd learned the greater delight of kissing them.

How she'd laughed. But then, that was Ruthie. She always laughed. How could he have forgotten? Fine. He hadn't forgotten, any more than he'd forgotten her generosity, her business acumen, her... He scowled. The bottomless faith she possessed that kept him from ever taking her for his wife.

They had been good together—like a key in a lock. But then that fateful day in Afghanistan had happened, shaking and even breaking the faith he'd lived by all his life. As a result, he'd lost an important part that had made them fit together so perfectly. Ever the optimist, she had believed they could work through the problem, but he hadn't wanted to lead her on when he knew that his foundering belief made them incompatible. He hadn't wanted to hurt her—to hurt either of them—with the hope that their differences could be overcome.

In order to protect her from his own traitorously weak will, he had turned away from her. Refused to answer her letters that asked questions for which he himself did not know the answers.

To be honest, it had been hard to lock away his feelings for Ruthie. To shove his emotions aside and move on, putting one foot in front of the other.

But that was then. He was a different person now, with different beliefs. His time in the army had taken him through some harsh experiences, led him to make some difficult decisions, but it had also taught him to get the assignment done, no matter what was going on inside his head and heart. Being around Ruthie meant he needed to barricade his heart. Not so much for himself as to protect her.

The inconvenient truth was that he still loved her. And for that reason, he could not let her know how much she still meant to him.

On the way to the hospital, Gray tried not to think about the woman in the passenger seat, so he used the short ride to fill her in on the details. Pop had left Naoko in the ground-floor bedroom for only a short time to prepare her favorite meal of udon noodles. When he returned with the lunch tray a short while later, Naoko's leg had become painful and swollen. Her doctor had warned them of potentially fatal complications after the hip surgery, so Pop had promptly called the rescue squad. A follow-up call revealed that they'd arrived at the hospital and Naoko had been whisked off for tests to see if the clot was starting to move. The worst-case possibility was that it could travel to her lungs and kill her.

When they arrived at the hospital, they were told she was being moved to a room to stay overnight. After she was settled in, someone would give them the room number. He led Ruthie to a quiet corner of the waiting room to wait for Pop to come tell them that Sobo was going to be fine. That was the hope anyway.

Gray leaned back in the waiting room chair and covered his eyes with the crook of his arm. He had no idea what had prompted him to swing by Abundance and pick up Ruthie. At the time, he had told himself it was because her presence would be a comfort to Pop. Gray could have just as easily told her the news and let her find her own way to the hospital, but some inner urge had propelled him to the store Ruthie had opened shortly after their breakup…compelled him to draw her close during this time of need.

Until now he'd been doing so well keeping his distance. Pretending he and Ruthie didn't mean anything to each other anymore. Now, with this one short exposure to the pretty redhead with the soft-spoken demeanor and gentle encouragement, the years and distance melted away. If he was honest with himself, he'd have to admit he needed her as much as Pop did.

Maybe more. The realization made him uncomfortable. For now, he'd stick with the excuse he'd given her on the car ride over here…that Sobo and Pop would want to see her after Sobo came out of the emergency room.

A few minutes later, he felt more than heard Ruthie get up from the couch beside him and pace the floor. Before that she'd been staring at her lap, her lips moving in silent prayer. He doubted her heartfelt pleas would do Sobo any good, but if the lifelong ritual brought Ruthie comfort, that was all that mattered.

"Pop's been gone a long time." Concern laced her smooth voice. "I thought all they had to do was wheel Sobo to the in-patient floor and Pop would come tell us her room number. They could have moved her to Tokyo and back by now."

He dropped his arm and sat upright. "They probably have to hook her up to drips and get her settled first. That always takes time."

Ruthie stopped pacing and returned to the seat beside him. "I'm glad you came for me," she said without looking at him. "Sobo and Pop mean a lot to me."

He studied her while she toyed with an old-fashioned amethyst ring on her right hand. Her left hand remained bare, leading him to wonder who she might be dating now. Although his grandparents occasionally mentioned her in passing, they always steered clear of information that might be too personal…or too painful.

"I know," he said softly. "And you mean a lot to them."

With her hazel gaze fixed on him, her steady assessment seemed to be more in response to what he didn't say than what actually came out of his mouth. To be fair to her, though, he wouldn't tell her the rest…that she also meant a lot to him.

Even if it was the truth.

He wished he could believe again. It would be so much simpler if he did. But after being abandoned by God during his time of greatest need—an event that had resulted in the death of a young man who'd counted on him and God for protection—Gray saw no point in pretending. And he refused to lie to Ruthie by letting her think he still believed. Why couldn't he be like other guys? Just tell a girl what she wanted to hear and reap the benefits of her affection. He could have easily continued on with their marriage plans and let her comfort him through the grief he'd endured in that hellish place called Afghanistan. But that wouldn't have been fair to her. And his daddy hadn't raised him that way.

Gray had been barely five years old when his father had pulled him aside prior to deployment to Saudi Arabia, explaining that during his absence Gray was to serve as the man of the family. "Your job is to take care of the people you love," he'd said with great seriousness. "Look after your mother and sister, even when you'd rather play with your race cars."

His father was retired from the army now and working in a civilian job, but Gray still carried the responsibility—the duty—to protect the ones he loved. Though he may have failed on occasion, it wasn't from lack of trying. His mouth tightened. There was one person he would never fail. No matter what it took, he'd protect her to the very best of his ability.

He'd never dreamed, though, that taking care of Ruthie would mean having to give her up.

* * *

In Naoko's room, Ruthie greeted Gray's parents and his sister, Catie, with hugs, then took a seat on the deep windowsill to leave room for the others. Gray sidled around to Ruthie's side of the bed and stood beside her. It was weird how his calm presence made her feel that all would turn out well.

Naoko's pulmonologist came in, listened to her lungs and proceeded to fill the family in on her condition.

"It's not unusual for patients to develop a thrombus after a hip fracture." The blond-haired doctor's shirt gapped at the neck, around which a tie had been tightened to take up the slack. He appeared to be just out of medical school, but he sounded very knowledgeable as he explained the risk from the clot that had developed near Naoko's surgery site. "A thrombus is a fancy word for blood clot. If it travels to the lungs, then it's called a pulmonary embolism, which is what we're concerned about right now."

Gray leaned forward and touched his grandmother's hand. "I thought the heparin she's been taking since surgery was supposed to prevent it."

"That was the hope, but it looks like she'll need something stronger to dissolve the clot. There are some side effects from the stronger medication, but surgery to remove the thrombus is even riskier. So we're going to keep her for several days to watch and wait for it to dissolve."

Ruthie's heart sank. She could read between those lines. It would be touch and go for the next few days until she was out of harm's way.

"No worries," Naoko said, her voice tired from the

strain of her ordeal. Her skin, normally a warm amber color, now held a grayish cast. Her fingers closed around her grandson's hand, and she pointed at the ceiling. "I am in God's hands. He will get me through."

Ruthie gave a silent prayer of thanks that Naoko was still with them. She had no doubt God had been with her all along. Her condition could have become much worse. Naoko wasn't out of the woods yet, but she would receive the benefit of the prayers of her and the family—*most* of the family—and the church.

She wondered whether Naoko's words were intended to assure the family or herself. Their effect on Gray, however, was clear. A muscle twitched along his temple, and he extended his hand to the doctor.

"Thank you for all you've done so far, Doctor."

They followed him into the hall and lingered together after the doctor left. Ruthie wanted to reassure Gray that, as Naoko had said, she was in God's hands. "Everyone who knows Sobo—and many who don't—will be praying for her," she said, laying a hand on his thick arm. "She's a strong woman, and God's healing touch will help her recover."

Gray turned his gaze away from her. "I'd rather count on the skill of the doctor and the medicine she's receiving. That's what will save her."

Ruthie reacted as if she'd been punched in the gut. In a manner of speaking, she had been. Church had been an important part of their upbringing, both hers and Gray's. Whenever healing occurred, it was understood that although physicians and medications were valuable tools in the process, true healing ultimately came from God. He was the one who gave the doctors wisdom and enabled the medicines to work. To deny

God's role in Sobo's recovery sounded to her ears as if Gray was offering his loved one up to the whims of chance and limited earthly abilities.

"Then I suppose we have all the bases covered," she said, letting him know without arguing the point that although he dismissed all but what he could see with his own eyes, she and the rest of the family would continue to put their faith in prayer.

He must certainly know, without her saying so, that God was the great healer. What he didn't know was that for the past four years she had prayed every day for God to heal Gray's shaken faith. Once her prayers were answered and Gray opened his heart enough to let God back in, she would ask God to make room in there for her, as well.

Chapter Two

"Thanks for your help yesterday, Paisley. I don't know what I would have done without you and Savannah pitching in to keep Gleanings open while I was at the hospital." Ruthie took a seat at the counter in Milk & Honey and gently pushed aside a ceramic Peter Rabbit to make room for her elbows.

Paisley moved behind the counter and flipped the switch to backlight what she called her higgledy-piggledy wall…shelves divided into cubes and filled with various sorts of teapots, spoon collections, antique cups, honeypots, snow globes and porcelain crumpet baskets. A British transplant, Paisley loved sharing bits of her homeland with customers.

In the seating area behind Ruthie, tables were given the illusion of privacy by separating them with low shelves strategically filled with packets of flavored teas, jars of jam, notecards, knickknacks, tea cozies and anything British to entice diners to take home a little memento of their Milk & Honey experience. Over to the side of the store, tucked away in locked display cases, were the real treasures—silver tea sets, rare water pitchers and ornate sugar bowls. The more unusual the better, and if the piece had an interesting story behind it, better still.

On the opposite side of the dining counter, Paisley lit the fire under a cast-iron skillet and set a glass of orange juice in front of Ruthie.

"No problem. I was happy to help," Paisley replied. Her accent always sounded so elegant and cultured. It was a huge draw for the customers. She refilled the coffee cup of an older gentleman sporting a white handlebar mustache and handed Ruthie a sheet featuring this week's specials. "We sold a few of Mr. Bristow's gewgaws yesterday, and a lovely Asian lady was quite excited about a quaint little Japanese doll she found."

The kissing dolls. Ruthie hadn't planned to keep them, but neither had she anticipated their sale would hit her so hard in the solar plexus.

"That's great," she said, her voice not quite matching Paisley's enthusiasm. "Was it Chou from the Tokyo Market down the street? Sobo loves to shop there."

"No, I've seen this lady a couple of times before, so I assume she's local, but I don't know who she is. Speaking of Mrs. Bristow, what's the latest on her status?"

Ruthie gave her a full update with the unfortunate news that the redness and swelling on Naoko's leg showed no improvement.

"She'll be fine," her friend reassured. Taking advantage of the momentary lull, she poured herself a cup of tea and flashed a guilty grin before she snitched one of the biscotti from the tin. "The whole church is praying for her. And besides, she's a tough lady. Remember the time when we were in university, and she climbed up on the roof of our house to replace some shingles?"

"Pop was furious when he found out. He kept going on about her falling and possibly getting a concussion." Ruthie took a sip of her freshly squeezed juice. "Come to think of it, that was his same concern when she fell off the rose trellis a couple of days ago. He kept telling her, 'Thank God you didn't crack your head.'"

"It's sweet, actually. He's madly protective of her."

The acorn didn't fall very far from the Bristow tree. In that regard Gray was a lot like his grandfather. Ruthie mentally kicked herself for letting her attention drift back to the man who still held the pieces of her broken heart in his strong hands.

She must have cracked her own head to think that she could pray her former fiancé back to God and to herself. But if God didn't give up on lost sheep, then she certainly wouldn't give up on Gray.

She focused on the specials menu, then looked over at Mustache Man at the end of the counter, who was digging into a hearty English breakfast. "What he's having looks good. Is that French toast?"

"Eggy bread? No."

Ruthie had never heard the refined Paisley snort before. This was a first.

"It's fried bread. I'll do a nice British fry-up for you, complete with egg, bacon, sausage, tomato and a dab of beans." She turned to the skillet and talked over her shoulder. "Now fess up. You've deliberately avoided telling me how you fared with Gray yesterday."

So much for taking her mind off him. Ruthie shrugged. "There's nothing to say. I'm not really sure what that was about, though. After these past six months avoiding each other, he suddenly wanted me at the hospital with him. Constantly."

It had been nice to be close to him after all this time apart, but also stressful because there had been so much left unsaid between them.

She fought to keep her voice strong, to look at Paisley directly when all she wanted was to bury her head in her arms and cry like a baby. But she was stronger than that now. She could do this. With effort she could convince Paisley and her friends that she no longer felt anything for Gray. Convincing her own heart was another matter.

"But after he drove me home," she continued, "he couldn't get out of there fast enough."

"Perhaps he wanted to kiss you goodbye and was just avoiding temptation." Paisley pulled a batch of scones from the oven, topped one with clotted cream and jam, set it on a scalloped-edge plate and carried it to a pair of women laughing at a corner table.

Ruthie choked back a laugh at her friend's comment. Big talk coming from a friend who studiously shied away from male attention. But then, Paisley had her reasons.

The minute they were alone again, Ruthie suggested, "Or maybe he didn't want to lead me on. Not that I'd be interested, of course."

"Of course." For some reason, the Brits did sarcasm far better than Americans. It had to be the accent. Paisley deftly changed the subject. "I heard Gray is planning corporate security systems now. What do you say we have him put one in here?"

"What do you say we let him continue to avoid me?"

"He didn't avoid you yesterday."

"The same could be said of your police officer friend."

Paisley set the fry-up in front of her and shot her a blue-eyed dagger. "Don't try to make something out of nothing."

Ruthie poked her fork at the delicious looking but heavy breakfast. "What do you put on fried bread?"

"Your teeth."

The front door chimed, and Paisley turned back to the smoking fry pan. She switched on the vent to draw out some of the smoke. A second later red-and-yellow flames danced along the surface of the overheated oil.

"Oh, my!" Paisley turned in a circle, apparently in search of something to put out the fire.

Ruthie scooted off her stool and ran behind the counter to help. The customer from the end of the counter followed on her heels.

"Get the baking soda!" Paisley cried.

The man snatched a can of something from the prep table.

"No, not that!" Ruthie lunged to grab the can out of his hand, but before she could reach it, he threw the contents on the flames.

Whoof! The pan flared up in a miniature fireball, and baking powder poofed everywhere.

In a panic, Ruthie debated what to do first...tend to Paisley, whose blunt-cut brunette bangs now frizzled like tiny electrified wires, get the customer with the melting handlebar mustache out of the kitchen before he did further damage or try to extinguish the pan before it caught something else on fire. Before she could make a move, someone pushed past her, turned off the gas flames and deftly slid a lid over the hot pan.

Gray, their fast-thinking rescuer, turned on the water, doused clean dish towels with cold water, offered them to the threesome and suggested they hold the cooling cloths to their faces to take away the sting of the heat.

Paisley touched a hand to her cheek. "I don't think I'm burned. Just a little warm."

After a quick check of the customer revealed a slight redness near his lip where his mustache wax had melted, Gray turned to Ruthie. He grabbed her by the upper arms and studied her intensely. First her face, then down to her hands, which he turned over to check for burns. She'd been farther away from the fire when it flashed, so she hadn't felt the effects of the heat. Yet even after he'd finished giving her the once-over, he held on. She wondered if he realized how tightly he gripped her upturned hands.

"Are you all right?" he asked, concern drawing a vertical line on his forehead.

"I'm fine," she said in a shaky voice, "but Paisley looks weird."

Along with her bangs, Paisley's eyebrow hairs had faded from dark brunette to pale brown and corkscrewed in all directions. Her cheeks and nose glowed a faint pink, but it wasn't clear whether the color came from a burn or stress.

Savannah dashed over from Connecting Threads, her blond hair bouncing on her shoulders.

"I heard a loud *whoosh* clear across the store," she said, "and when I looked over here, it seemed as though the whole place had gone up like a dried-out Christmas tree."

While Savannah bustled from one friend to the other and then the older man, double-checking them for heretofore unnoticed signs of injury, Gray quietly herded the ensemble out of the kitchen.

"It's a miracle no one was hurt," Savannah declared. "God must have been watching over y'all."

Gray fixed his gaze on Ruthie, his expression making it clear he would not be joining in the choruses of "praise God."

"We need to talk," he said.

While her friends cleaned up the kitchen, Ruthie followed Gray back to the Gleanings area. Several new finds awaited price tags, and boxes from the Bristow house still sat near the checkout counter where she had left them yesterday afternoon. There were not yet any customers at this early hour of the morning.

A terrible thought raced through her heart. "Sobo. Did the clot—?"

"She's the same," he said, moving his hands as if to erase whatever worry she might have. "It's not about her."

Relief flooded through her. But the troubled expression on Gray's face killed the momentary reprieve. Were they finally going to confront the awkward elephant that had stood between them for the past four years? Worse, was he going to tell her he'd moved on and found someone else?

"It's about Pop."

Ruthie touched a hand to her mouth. "Oh, no."

"No, not Pop, but his stuff. You haven't already sold the things he brought in yesterday, have you?"

His dark brow furrowed together, and he jammed his hands into his jeans pockets in a sign that Ruthie had come to know meant something was bothering him. Apparently, this was about more than just a few collectible doodads.

"I don't think so." She looked inside the half dozen open boxes sitting on and beside the counter. "These haven't been inventoried yet, but it looks like everything's still here."

She paused, remembering what Paisley had said about selling the kissing dolls. Had he come back for them? Did they hold the same meaning for him that they did for her?

"Oh, wait. There was one thing, a pair of knick-knacks that used to sit on the piano."

She watched him, but his intense gaze never flickered. He didn't remember? Her heart sank a little.

He shook his head. "One of the boxes was full of military stuff from Pop's service in Korea. Awards and medals, pictures, journals. Some keepsakes. He had set that box aside to put away but brought it to you by mistake."

"Don't worry, I'm sure it's here somewhere."

They started with the stack beside the counter. Few of the contents matched the kinds of things Ruthie sold at Gleanings. She usually focused on antique or unusual one-of-a-kind items bought from estate sales and moving sales, but these would be sold on consignment for the Bristows. The idea had been to spare Pop the trouble of organizing a yard sale when he needed to take care of Sobo. He'd initially pushed aside the stored items in the spare bedroom to make room for Sobo's rented hospital bed. But his wife's Japanese decorating taste won out, and soon the room looked as sparse and clean as the rest of the house.

They went through the three stacked boxes of odds

and ends first, then moved a fourth from the small pedestal table Pop had brought and set it on the counter. The tabletop's inlaid design of golden-colored grain beckoned her to trace her fingers around the bent heads of barley.

She clearly remembered sitting at this table on the Bristows' screened porch, playing Jenga with Gray and his younger sister while a warm summer breeze blew over the trio. Gray had stared intently at the stacked wooden blocks, determined to remove a piece without collapsing the precarious tower. Ruthie had laughed at his seriousness over the silly game, but he'd just refocused his concentration. With a hint of mischief guiding her actions, she'd touched her bare toes to the twisted barley pedestal and given it a nudge so slight the crashing of the tower could have easily been blamed on the breeze.

When his foot came down on hers, she'd suspected she'd been caught. Instead, he'd conceded defeat and promptly invited her to the Byrd Theatre for a 99-cent second-run movie. It was their first date, and he'd held her hand during the entire time the Wurlitzer organ played before the movie started. Ruthie had no memory of the movie, but she could still remember the exact feel of her hand in his, the calluses on his palm scratching her skin. Remembered wishing they hadn't bought popcorn each time he let go to reach into the carton for a handful of the buttery stuff.

It had been part of the best time of her life. The laughter. The fun. Sharing new experiences together. The discovery that, no matter what activity they engaged in, it was always better when they did it together. And most of all, there was the easy camaraderie. The feeling that they could say or do anything without self-consciousness or censoring.

The rest of the family seemed to approve of their nearly constant togetherness. Since Gray's parents lived only a few blocks away, it had been easy for him to slip away frequently and come to visit her under the guise of checking on his grandparents. And on occasion, Ruthie would walk over to visit his younger sister, but spend as much or more time with Gray.

But now…well, she measured every word she spoke and guarded every glance she sent his way. It was an uncomfortable balancing act between keeping a circumspect distance and wanting to slip back into that easy way of relating they used to have.

"I knew you shook the table," he said, breaking into her moment of reverie. He gave her a nostalgic grin edged with regret.

Or maybe she was just hoping for a twinge of regret.

"Then why didn't you say something?"

He gave a soft chuckle. "I liked your determination to win."

"Even if my methods were a little hinky?"

He put his hand on hers, bridging the present with the past. "I'm sorry for hurting you. For telling you something so intense in a letter instead of…"

"Instead of by Skype?" she finished for him. The comment had been intended to refer to the thousands of miles separating them at the time, but it came out sounding bitter.

Something between an apology and a grimace crossed his face. "Yeah, I guess even that would have been more personal. More face-to-face."

He looked away and removed his hand from hers, taking the warmth with it.

"And I guess it was pretty cowardly of me to keep dodging you after I came back home, but I convinced myself it was to protect you from an awkward meeting at my grandparents'." He returned his attention to her, meeting her gaze directly. "What I'm trying to say is, I'm sorry for the way I handled things."

Sure, it had been unpleasant, but what breakup wasn't? Even if they'd been in the same room, it wouldn't have hurt any less. Despite her own pain, she knew whatever had caused him to change his mind about God and a future with her must have been hurting him much, much more.

She shook her head. "No apology necessary," she said. "That's all in the past now."

We're in the past, she almost added.

"You may not be a Bristow by marriage," he continued, "but according to my grandparents, you're still family. We're going to see each other at family events, so we need to be able to put the awkwardness aside. For Pop and Sobo's sake, if not our own."

Ruthie nodded and offered him a wistful smile. "Yeah, it's been hard juggling holidays and drop-by visits for the times you're not there."

"So I'm not the only coward," he teased. He pulled a cardboard box closer to him and lifted a flap. "Maybe we should meet for lunch sometime. Clear the air about the past and set up ground rules for the future."

"Rules of engagement, you mean."

He flinched as if she'd hit him.

She'd intended it in the military sense, of course, but

it was only after seeing his reaction that she realized her words could be taken a different way.

"I'm sorry. I didn't mean—"

"It's okay," he said with a forced smile. "Maybe we could call them rules of *disengagement*."

The joke wasn't funny, so she didn't laugh.

The door opened, and a stylish young mother with a baby in a stroller entered the building. The woman spotted the Gleanings sign over the counter and headed toward the shop to browse.

"Feel free to look around," Ruthie told her. "And let me know if you have any questions."

Gray's expression quickly changed to one of relief. "Here it is. Pop's Korean War stuff."

"That's great." Ruthie bent to look at the assortment of papers, medals, photos and sentimental trinkets. "We get history hunters in here all the time. Pop would be heartbroken if we'd sold all those memories."

He closed the box flaps. "Thanks. For this," he said, gesturing toward the mementos. "For everything."

At her questioning glance, he added, "For being there for Pop and Sobo while I was away."

"Your parents were there for them," she said, deflecting his praise. "They looked after them."

"Yes, but you gave Sobo and Pop someone other than me to focus on. You made a difficult time in their lives a little more tolerable."

She shook off his thanks. "They've been there for me more than I was for them. I don't know what I would have done—where I would have gone—if they hadn't stepped in when I needed help most."

Gray's expression took on a faraway look. Was he

thinking of God—who he'd said wasn't there when he'd needed help most?

He tucked the box of Pop's treasures under one arm and laid some bills on the counter. Then he moved the small, round table closer to the door. "I'll take the table, too. Is this enough to cover it?"

"Way too much. You could buy a new one for less." She wondered if the table had stirred memories for him as it had for her.

He must have read her mind. "There's a bare spot in the corner of my kitchen. This should fit just about right." With the box still tucked under his arm, he picked up the table with the other hand and moved toward the door. He stopped and turned back to her. "Don't tell Pop and Sobo I bought it, or they'll try to pay me back."

"Let me give you a hand."

Either the box or the table alone would have been manageable, but the weight of both was clearly an effort for him. She came from around the counter, but he hefted the table closer.

"Thanks, but I've got it."

With a resigned sigh, Ruthie stood back and watched him struggle through the door, determined to carry his burden alone.

The fire at Milk & Honey was nearly forgotten when the lunch crowd poured in. By that afternoon, Savannah had sold a vintage dress to a teen for her upcoming prom, and Nikki, who helped run the shop next door and who they hoped would be a future partner at Abundance someday, had taken apart an antique typewriter to repair and restore.

Whenever Ruthie thought about how Abundance and the individual shops within it came to be, she thanked God for bringing together the original three talented friends who, each in her own way, loved to find interesting articles and offer them for sale, and then adding a fourth to the mix. She sometimes laughingly called Savannah and Paisley her "Craigslist friends," since it had been an online ad seeking roommates that had brought them together in the first place. Then, after moving into their Abundance shops, they'd been blessed to meet Nikki, who worked next door.

The college years had been lean for the three friends, so they'd sought to decorate the rented house with flea market and thrift-store finds. Ruthie started them off with unusual pieces of antique furniture hidden under ugly coats of paint or dulled varnish, which she refinished and made to look like new. Savannah found lovely old tablecloths, bedspreads and dresses that showed small signs of wear and fashioned them into beautiful curtains fit for a showroom. And Paisley, with her penchant for food and hospitality, supplied fancy plates and introduced the group to the likes of tea infusers, egg-poaching cups and soup tureens.

Visitors were always astonished to see how stylish they'd made the place look with little or no money. Soon friends, family and acquaintances were asking the threesome to find specific items, and before long their individual hobbies had grown into businesses that helped pay for their college expenses. This was a blessing, especially since Ruthie wanted to pay her own way and avoid drawing further on the Bristows' kindness after all they'd done for her over the years.

After graduation, the three friends decided to combine their businesses under a single roof they called Abundance. The exception was Nikki, who worked next door at the Carytown shoe repair shop, called Restore My Sole. When the ancient owner, Jericho Jones, discovered her talent for fixing things, he began accepting repair jobs for small items and gave the tasks to her to complete. And when the space next door became available for rent just before the others' college graduation, Nikki became an unofficial fourth member of the Abundance friendship. Nikki's loyalty to Jericho kept her working for him, but they used the connecting door between the stores whenever the Abundance shop owners needed their friend's skills to restore acquired treasures prior to sale.

Between waiting on customers, Ruthie tackled the remaining boxes from the Bristows and kept an eye open for any other war memorabilia that might have made their way into the wrong place. To her delight, and especially Savannah's, one of the boxes contained several ladies' hats that appeared to be from the early sixties.

"I need your help pricing them," Ruthie said after she'd taken the find over to Connecting Threads.

Her friend turned them over and checked for a label. She gasped. "These were made by the Hat Factory down in Shockoe Slip. Back in their heyday, before the factory went out of business, it was *the* local place for ladies to buy hats. You shouldn't have any trouble finding buyers for these."

Judging by the way Savannah practically drooled

over them, Ruthie wouldn't be surprised if her friend bought one herself.

Savannah's fingers followed the loose band of a particularly pretty go-to-church hat, and she twisted her lips into a slight frown. "The puggaree is loose. I'll fix it for you so no one will have any reason to turn this beauty down." Savannah perched the hat on her head and peered into the floor mirror. With a hand on her hip and a point of the toe, she struck a saucy pose. "Mrs. Bristow sure had good taste."

Ruthie agreed. "Pop said that shortly after he brought her here from Tokyo, she studied fashion magazines and bought American clothes to try to fit in." Naoko had even adopted her husband's faith as her own and now hated to miss a single Sunday at church. "She still looks stylin', even when she's just puttering around the house."

"You'd never guess she's pushing eighty."

Savannah set the hat with the loose band on top of her sewing pile, then helped Ruthie tag the remaining hats with prices that should be high enough to reflect their value but not high enough to scare off potential customers.

Ruthie thanked her and took the hats back to Gleanings, where she displayed them on the Peg-Board wall behind her counter. Then she pulled out the box she'd been sorting just before Gray's unexpected arrival yesterday. Tucked between an early transistor radio and a pair of binoculars was the pair of kissing dolls…right where she'd left them.

She frowned, remembering the conversation she'd had with Paisley this morning. How could Paisley have sold the dolls if they were still here?

* * *

Three times in two days. This was more than Gray had seen Ruthie over the past four years. And it was taking a toll on him.

Sleep had eluded him last night while he worried about Naoko. When he did sleep, his dreams had been filled with images of Ruthie. The way her hands fluttered like a butterfly without a road map whenever she talked. That soft reddish-brown hair that begged him to touch it. And the hazel eyes that telegraphed every emotion that crossed her heart.

He found her at the rear of the shop, her back turned to him while she focused her attention on straightening a three-foot-wide metal disc on the wall, and he took advantage of her distraction to study her.

She wore slim khaki pants topped by a pale green shirt that made her hair seem more red than brown. Her movements were more confident now than four years ago, possibly the result of proving herself to be an accomplished businesswoman. Ruthie had always been a hard worker. And her devotion had obviously paid off, judging by the shoppers milling around him who exclaimed to their friends over the items they discovered.

It must have been hard for her, losing her mother in the middle of her teen years. Though Ruthie had never said anything against her stepfather, Gray had picked up from his grandparents' conversations that when the new widower spent a Saturday packing the house to move him and his biological daughter back to New Jersey, the man had turned to Ruthie and asked, "Where are you going to live?"

At church the following day, Naoko had noticed Ruthie's tears after silent prayer time. Until that day, their relationship had consisted mostly of friendly hellos. His grandmother couldn't stand to see anyone hurting, so she'd pulled Ruthie aside and learned that the girl's only blood relatives—a chronically ill aunt and a cousin with a drug problem—could not take her in. With nowhere else to turn, her only other option was foster care.

In less than twenty-four hours, his grandparents had moved her into their house and applied to become Ruthie's legal guardians. How could someone hurt her like that? And then it hit him. *He* had hurt her like that. He had rejected her, just like her family. The thought threatened to rip him apart. Of course, he'd done it to protect her. Somehow he doubted she saw it that way.

Ruthie stepped away from hanging the oversize replica of an antique coin and appeared to notice him out of the corner of her eye. She smiled and turned to greet him. Gray smiled back, hoping his guilt didn't bleed through his expression. When her gaze fully met his, the smile dissipated. Or maybe she caught some hint of what he'd been feeling.

"I just spoke with Sobo," she said, as if clearing off that reason for his sudden reappearance. "She's not crazy about the hospital food."

"Maybe it needs soy sauce," he joked. "It's good she feels well enough to want to eat."

Ruthie nodded agreement and waited. He sensed her unspoken question. *Why have you come back?*

"There was a doll," he said, getting to the point. "It had been in the box with Pop's military stuff." He drew a deep breath, hoping they might find it in one of the cartons they hadn't searched earlier today. "Sobo needs it. Pop said it has special meaning for her."

Ruthie relaxed her guarded stance, pulled her pony-tail loose, then refashioned it. "Good news. It wasn't sold after all." With a tilt of her head, she added, "I wasn't aware it meant so much to her. She always said she didn't like *ranzatsu*."

Her easy pronunciation of the Japanese word for clutter drew a spontaneous grin from him. Relieved she still had the doll in her possession, he hoped this would be the last time he would need to come back for a while. Although they had called a truce and would no longer need to avoid each other at family gatherings, he thought it best to ease back into contact with her. And preferably with his grandparents around to act as a buffer.

"Well, clutter is the last thing she'd call this doll. It's the only thing she has left from her childhood."

"No problem. They're right over here."

They? He followed her to the counter where most of the boxes had been emptied and set aside for later use. Pop had mentioned only one doll.

"Did the table fit?" She set a small cardboard box on the counter and reached inside.

"Like it was designed for the house." It looked great in the corner of his kitchen, but he still wondered at the impulse that had driven him to buy it. Now he'd think of Ruthie every morning at breakfast…and remember the look of mischief on her face and the touch of her bare toes against his foot.

She handed him a pair of porcelain dolls, their lips puckered for a kiss.

He turned them over in his hands and stared at them, remembering the time early in their relationship when their own actions mimicked the dolls'. Drawing his and Ruthie's features on them had provided the perfect opener for their first kiss. And many more after that.

"What happened to the freckles?"

She flashed him another of her sassy grins. "Foundation makeup. It covers a lot of flaws."

He knew she was joking, but the comment drew his attention to her face. The cute little specks were still there, but much lighter now, and he couldn't help wondering if there were still twenty-nine. Somehow he doubted she'd let him count them. Perhaps spending less time in the sun had allowed them to fade. He hoped she wasn't trying to cover them with makeup.

She ducked her head and looked away under his scrutiny. He hadn't meant to bring out her shyness, but he couldn't let her put herself down, even if only in jest.

"I don't consider freckles flaws," he said, and idly ran a thumb over the girl doll's puckered face.

Mirroring his gesture, Ruthie lifted a hand to her face, then immediately slid her hand into her slacks pocket.

"Right. They're kiss prints," she said, automatically parroting back the words he used to tell her.

She looked uncomfortable, as if realizing she'd opened a door that led someplace they weren't supposed to go. "I'm sure Sobo will be glad to get this set back," she said, abruptly changing the subject.

Gray shook his head. "This isn't the doll I'm looking for. The one I'm talking about is the size of a Barbie and has real hair and a red kimono."

Ruthie sagged against the counter. "Oh, no."

"Oh, no?" He clutched the porcelain dolls tighter. "What does 'oh, no' mean?"

"That must have been the doll that was sold. I thought Paisley meant *these*."

She looked sick, and that was the way Gray felt right now.

"You *sold* it?"

She gave a slow nod and pinched her lip between small white teeth. "Yesterday, while we were at the hospital. Paisley said an Asian woman bought it. I hadn't inventoried all of the boxes at that point, so I assumed she was talking about the kissing dolls."

With a knot in the pit of his stomach, Gray considered the possibilities. Pop had said Naoko treasured that doll, and he didn't want her to come home from the hospital to find that her most valued possession had been sold. He pushed the kissing dolls into Ruthie's hands. "Sobo has to have it," he insisted. "Call the customer and get it back."

"I don't know who bought it." Her voice sounded precariously close to cracking. "It was a cash sale."

He closed his eyes and wiped a hand over his face, wishing he could wipe away the problem. "Sobo doesn't care much about…things," he said. He almost said *worldly* things, which was the way she always phrased it, but something made him leave that part out. "This is the one item she treasures, and if there's any way to get it back for her, I'm going to do it."

"I know." Ruthie wrung her hands, then retightened her ponytail. "I feel just terrible about it. Sobo has been so good to me. If there was any way I could find her doll…"

"There is," he said, taking the kissing dolls from her and placing them on the counter. He dropped his hands on her shoulders and pulled her toward him.

"We'll put our heads together. Between the two of us, we should be able to cover all possible bases. From this point on, you and I will be joined at the hip until Sobo's doll is found."

Chapter Three

At the Bristows' house that evening, Pop took Ruthie and Gray to the downstairs guest room to show them the progress he'd made clearing out excess odds and ends accumulated over the years. Ruthie used the short delay to try to decide the best way to break the news to him.

Since sleeping upstairs was out of the question for a while, an adjustable twin bed had been pushed against the far wall for Sobo during her recovery from hip surgery. A recliner had been moved in here from the den, presumably where Pop would sleep, and Ruthie was touched by the devotion he held for his wife.

Her dream was that someday she would have someone who would love her that much, even after fifty years together. She glanced over at Gray, who ran his hand over a glass-front display case.

"You did a great job clearing out this room, Pop," he said. "Sobo will be very happy."

Indeed he had. The clean design of the room reflected Naoko's Japanese heritage and minimalism. Simple shades for the windows, a small wool rug beside the bed, a nightstand and a dresser adorned with painted branches of cherry blossoms.

Pop smiled and puffed out his chest. The action made him seem more like a young boy than a white-haired man in his early eighties. "No *ranzatsu* in here," he said. "That case will eventually go in the den, where we'll display my army things and her doll. Memories of when we met. But for now they'll stay in here." He grew oddly quiet for a moment. Finally, he said, "She needs to see them."

Although Ruthie had been close to the Bristows for eleven years and had asked Sobo on various occasions about their romantic beginnings, she still didn't know how the pair had met. The elderly woman had deflected her questions with a bow of her head and started talking about one of the household projects she always had going. Ruthie made a mental note to ask Pop about it at a more appropriate time.

He laid a hand on Gray's shoulder and squeezed. "Give me a hand to move it over here, where she'll be able to see everything from the bed."

After the men maneuvered the furniture into position came the moment she and Gray had been dreading. Breaking the news to Pop.

"About the doll," Gray began. "It's, uh, temporarily misplaced. It may be a while before we can get it back to you."

Ruthie had never known him to tap-dance around a subject the way he had just now.

"A while? Your grandmother will need it here when she comes home from the hospital. In a few days, God willing." A worried frown lined his brow. "And what do you mean by temporarily misplaced?"

Ruthie looped her hand through the crook of Pop's arm and they all walked to the kitchen. "I appreciate Gray for not laying blame at my feet," she said, "but the truth is that the doll was mistakenly sold from my shop. It's my fault for not setting your boxes aside until I finished taking inventory of them." She hated to disappoint him and avoided looking at the wounded expression in Pop's pale blue eyes while she filled him in on how the doll came to be sold.

He patted her arm. "If anyone is to blame, it's my own silly self for taking the wrong box to your store. How could you have known any different?"

"I promise you, I will do everything in my power to get it back."

Gray reached into a drawer near the sink and withdrew a pad of paper and a pen, then set them in front of Ruthie. "We should create a strategy list. Make sure we cover all the bases."

Ruthie started by listing what they'd already done to try to find the doll's purchaser. "One. Go through my customer list and start making calls to see if one of them might be our mystery lady. Two. Ask the neighboring business owners if they recognize the description Paisley gave of her."

Pop sat beside her at the table and touched a finger to the paper. "Did you pray?"

She smiled at the gentle reminder. "Of course. It should have gone at the top of the list—that's the first thing I did."

"Me, too."

He hugged her and cut a glance at Gray, who paced the floor like a military strategist planning a covert operation.

"Let's pull the security tapes from your store," he said, pausing in midstride. "That should give us a picture of the customer who bought the doll."

Ruthie slumped in her chair. "That's a great idea, but unfortunately, Abundance doesn't have a security camera." At the pained look on Gray's face, she quickly added, "Yet," but it was Pop who decided to belabor the point.

"You should have a camera in the store. And an alarm system connected to a dispatcher." He leaned toward her, concern underscoring his words. "I meant to tell you this earlier—there was a report on *News at Noon* today about a prowler on Strawberry Street. I want you and your friends to be protected in case someone should take a notion to break in."

"Strawberry Street is a good distance away, so I'm sure we won't have to worry about that person bothering the shop." The reports of someone lurking around homes and small stores had actually been closer to the house on Floyd Avenue that she still rented from the Bristows, but she wasn't about to bring that up. "Even so, I'll mention to Savannah and Paisley that we should beef up our security."

An idea occurred to her.

"Maybe Restore My Sole or one of the other shops near Abundance has a surveillance video of the parking lot. We might be able to get an image of the customer or, better yet, the number from her license plate."

"If she drove," Gray pointed out.

He was right. Many of their customers came from nearby residential areas such as Ellwood Avenue, which ran parallel to Cary Street behind their shop and was within easy walking distance. Or they were local employees who strolled over during their breaks or after work.

"I'll come by tomorrow after work to check out any videos your neighbors may have." He paused as if considering what he was about to say next. "And I'll do a walk-through of Abundance to determine what kind of security system will work best for your setup."

A lot had changed between them, but the one thing that remained the same about Gray was his fierce protectiveness. They might not be a couple anymore, but she knew that wouldn't stop him from doing everything in his power to keep her safe.

"You really don't need to go to the trouble," she assured him. "I'm sure we'll be fine until I make an appointment for someone to install an alarm."

Gray's engineering degree had been put to use securing facilities and equipment during his time in the army. Since his return home, he'd parlayed that experience into a thriving business designing and installing security systems for businesses and government offices. Asking him to outfit her little shop with a security camera and alarm would be like using a howitzer to kill a fly.

He ripped the list off the pad of paper and stuffed it in her hand. She moved to pull away, but he held her in his grip.

"Don't delay," he warned. "Wishing and hoping are not enough to keep you safe."

Once again, his protective side was showing. The odds of the prowler making an unwanted appearance at the Abundance shops were slim, but when Gray was in defender mode, arguing with him was pointless.

And though he didn't say it, his meaning came through loud and clear.

Prayers aren't enough, either.

That night in bed, Ruthie's prayers weren't enough to take her thoughts off Gray and his steadfast resistance to all things related to faith and the Bible. Like a cold-case investigator who keeps searching for clues in years-old evidence, she reached into her nightstand drawer and withdrew the letter that he'd sent her from Afghanistan. The paper, now tattered, held a place in her Bible in the book of Ruth.

That Wednesday night at church, she'd been excited when Sobo had handed her the old-fashioned letter from her sweetheart and her family and friends had watched expectantly as she'd read it. Something had felt wrong in the first sentence when he'd told her, "I'm sending this letter by way of my grandparents so you won't be alone when you read what I have to say."

Even now, four years later, a rock still formed in the pit of her stomach whenever she read those troubling words. But just as she had done back then, she forced herself to continue.

Something happened that has caused me to question my beliefs. I won't burden you by sharing the things I've seen, but suffice it to say that God—if there is such a being—let me down when I needed Him most. While I've been wrestling with this bad blow over the past few months, you've been steadfastly sending encouraging letters and emails. You must have sensed I was going through a tough time, so you tried to cheer me up and urged me

to lean on God. I love you, and I loved receiving
each and every one of your notes, but they only
served to illustrate how far apart we've grown.

She teared up at the knowledge that whatever had
caused Gray to lose his faith was something he would
not—perhaps could not—discuss with her or anyone
else. Pop, a veteran of the Korean War, had urged her
to give Gray time. Give him time to sort through the
unspeakable experiences he'd endured.

But how much time would it take? For his sake, she
prayed he would find answers to the questions that
troubled him.

She forced herself to read that paragraph again,
knowing the answer to Gray's trouble lay in his belief that God had abandoned him at a time when he
needed Him most.

Just as it had done that fateful night, the sound of
blood pounded in her ears, nearly deafening her, and
she became aware that her breathing was fast and shal-
low. Steeling herself to the pain that still stabbed every
time she read his words, she sucked in a deep breath
and blinked back the moisture that clouded her vision.

Although I'm not sure how I feel about God right
now, I do believe there's something to the warn-
ing in the Bible about being yoked together with
unbelievers. I love you and know how much you
love the Lord, but I can't pretend to believe so I
can be with you. It's not fair to either of us.

Like a passerby at a horrible traffic accident, all she
could do was continue to stare at the page in front of
her and read what came next.

It may hurt now, and believe me when I say it hurts me more than I can express, but it's best for both of us if I release you from our engagement so you can find someone else. Someone whose faith is as strong as your own.

You're a good person, Ruthie, and you deserve someone who won't hold you back. I'll understand if you hate me for this, but I will always care for you, even though we can't be together. I wish you much love and happiness.
Gray

A fist clenched around Ruthie's throat, and once again the room threatened to close in on her. She refolded the letter and returned it to the drawer, as if that simple action might take away the fresh pain that hit her every time she read it.

Hate was something she could never feel for Gray. Anguish, confusion, yes. Although she didn't fully comprehend the reason behind his change of heart, she'd never doubted his motives to do what he considered best for both of them.

Too numb to cry again, she leaned back against the pillow and pressed her hands to her forehead. Because of her faith, she had lost favor with Gray—the man she'd believed, and still did believe, that God intended for her.

With the Bible resting on her lap, she returned the letter to mark the pages of the book of Ruth.

"Please bring him back, Lord," she said. "To You and to me."

The following evening after the shops closed, Gray pocketed the parking lot surveillance tape he'd collected from the neighboring classic-auto supply store and walked through the Abundance building to search for possible security problems. His civilian career involved planning high-end security systems for large businesses and government agencies, which might have been the reason Ruthie had tried to decline his offer to set up a system here. But he suspected her reluctance was less about the size of the job, a departure from his usual contracts, and more about him.

After he was done with this, he'd cut out of here and go watch the tape. With a little luck, maybe it would offer up not only an image of the woman who'd bought his grandmother's doll but also a clear view of her car's license tag.

Ruthie and her friends buzzed around Milk & Honey in preparation for an evening neighborhood event.

Nikki walked by with an armload of food and plopped a plate of finger sandwiches in his hands. "Mind giving me a hand with this? We'll just set them on the table out back."

He followed her outside, where a few Ellwood Avenue neighbors from across the alley had begun gathering. A cheerful yellow cloth covered the imperfections of a beat-up picnic table. A couple of pitchers of sweet tea and lemonade sat at one end, so he set the plate of sandwiches at the opposite end with the meat pies, cookies and banana pudding.

"Oh, good. You're staying for our Sunset Blessings gathering." Paisley stuck an empty paper plate in his hands. "Help yourself. There's plenty of food."

Blessings? He'd already managed to bow out of attending the church prayer group last night after visiting Naoko with Pop and Ruthie. And he had no desire to attend a neighborhood kumbaya meeting, even if it did involve delicious-looking food.

"I don't— I mean…"

Ruthie seemed to sense his discomfort and attempted to reassure him. "Sunset Blessings is just an opportunity for us to be grateful at the end of the day for all we have and to share our abundance with others. Paisley started it by saving leftover goodies from Milk & Honey for people in need. It eventually grew to include our residential and business neighbors. Now everybody brings a little something, and folks enjoy not having to cook a couple of nights a week."

That was when he noticed the "people in need." A scruffy-looking pair of men and a girl who appeared to be in her teens joined the group with hellos and nods. The girl set a plastic cup with white flowers on the table, and the men waited for the ladies to help themselves to the food before filling their own plates.

They seemed harmless enough, but Gray decided it might be a good idea to stick around and see who else showed up. Though he commended Paisley and the others for sharing their bounty with those less fortunate, he couldn't help worrying that the free offerings might draw vagrants and other disreputable types.

Paisley cleared her throat and raised a hand for attention. Once all had quieted, she bowed her head and spoke in a clear tone. "Lord, thank You for this food. Please bless it, bless our neighbors and bless Daisy on her upcoming job interview. Amen."

Gray stared at the ground during the blessing, thinking not about what she said but about how she sounded so conversational, as if she and God were close friends. A moment of sadness speared his chest. Once upon a time, he'd had that sort of relationship. A relationship where he'd felt confident his prayers were heard and would be answered.

He raised his head, and the others applauded the job-seeking girl, who blushed under all the attention.

Ruthie leaned in and touched his arm. "Daisy's mother is no longer in the picture, and her father, Mark, was laid off last year and can only get occasional day jobs. They've been living in his car, but he insists Daisy finish high school. She's hoping to start working the day after graduation so she can afford an apartment for both of them."

He nodded, sympathizing with their predicament. "That must have been a tough decision. Choosing between her education and sleeping in a car or dropping out of school to work so they can sleep in a real bed."

She indicated the older middle-aged man with a scraggly goatee who accompanied the father-daughter pair. "That's Yard Dog. No one knows his real name. Paisley's very fond of him, and we think he's the reason she started this Sunset Blessings tradition."

As unofficial host of the group, Paisley started a round of introductions. "And this is Gray Bristow, Ruthie's—" Her eyes opened wide and she nervously pushed her hair behind her ear. "Her, um…"

"Family friend," Ruthie supplied.

To anyone else her smile looked easy and relaxed. But Gray saw the tense lines at the corners of her mouth. People continued eating and chatting without a clue about the undercurrents between them.

What was he doing here? The more time he spent with Ruthie, the more time he wanted to spend with her. He had told himself the reason he stuck around this evening was to protect her from any unsavory types who might be drawn to the free food. But he was here because, deep down inside, he was drawn to Ruthie and all the goodness that was wrapped up in the total package. In truth, *he* was the one he should be protecting her from.

What he loved most about her was her unwavering faith…in God, in people, in the underdog. But if they were together again, his own lack of faith would weaken hers. Would weaken the fabric of who she was.

He should keep his distance. For her sake, if not his own. After they found Naoko's doll, that was exactly what he would do. Stay a safe distance away. But right now she stood so close he could smell her shampoo. She smelled sweet, like apples, and reminded him of the fall weekends she and Naoko had spent preserving fruit from the tree in their backyard. As a young boy, he had always tried to avoid the hot, laborious canning duty that usually turned into a family event. But after Ruthie's arrival, he had often "dropped by" and ended up spending the entire day helping out just so he could be in her company.

He finished off the food on his plate. No time like the present. But before he could say his goodbyes, a mounted police officer rode up and joined the group. Judging by the way everyone greeted him, he was a regular at the Sunset Blessings festivities.

Ruthie filled him in. "That's Officer Worth. He rides by here after his shift almost every day to—" she made quote marks with her fingers "—keep an eye on things. We all think he has his eye on Paisley, but she acts more interested in his horse than in him."

Sure enough, Nikki offered the officer a plate of

food, and Paisley offered the horse an apple that she had already cut up for it.

Gray noticed the looks that passed between Ruthie and her friends. They were the same looks the others had exchanged each time he came to the shop.

Worth dismounted, but before he dug into the food, he cautioned everyone to be alert to any suspicious activity. Apparently, the prowler Pop had told them about last night had been spotted within a block of their shops.

"The break-ins occurred almost a mile away," he said, "so the sightings in this neighborhood may have been a result of overactive imaginations. But better safe than sorry. Be sure to call and report any suspicious activity."

Despite his words of assurance, a ripple of concern ran through the crowd.

A short while later, they began packing up, and leftovers were placed in plastic carryout containers conveniently left there by Paisley. Yard Dog and Mark gratefully accepted some of the extras.

Savannah waved to Daisy. "Don't go yet. I want to show you this fabulous dress I found for your interview."

Ruthie accompanied them inside, and Gray followed a few minutes later. By the time he joined them at Connecting Threads, Daisy had gone into the small bathroom located beyond the Milk & Honey kitchen and Savannah had retreated to the sewing machine at the back of her shop to thread the machine and make a small alteration to the dress.

He hated to come off as if he was judging the girl, but he finally gave in and voiced his concern. "Do you think it's a good idea to let her go back there unsupervised? Your offices and the safe—"

Ruthie lifted a hand to stop his protest. "Daisy is a regular girl caught up in a difficult situation. I don't think she'll touch anything she wasn't invited to."

It was times like this when Gray worried that Ruthie had too much faith in others. Especially this particular underdog.

"Besides, the safe is locked," she added, calming his concerns for the moment. "Sometimes I think you worry too much."

Of course he worried. He'd experienced things most people had only seen on TV. To others, the bad things that could happen in life were merely a hypothetical possibility. To him, they were reality.

"We may be just 'family friends,'" he said, referring to her description of their current relationship, "but I still care about you—and your friends—and don't want anything bad to happen to any of you."

She touched his wrist again. Every time she did that, he wanted to draw her into his arms and hold her as if nothing had ever come between them. But he couldn't. It wouldn't be fair to either of them to pretend that their differing beliefs could be overcome with a hug and wishful thinking.

"Have faith in us." She stepped away, though he sensed her reluctance. "We'll be fine."

That was something he couldn't do. He didn't have faith in her abilities or in God to protect her. She was so trusting. So willing to believe the best about people. Fear dug at his heart, and he worried what might happen if she or her friends should encounter the prowler

Officer Worth warned them about. Would Ruthie know what to do? Would she know how to protect herself?

He'd learned a few things during his time in the army. Some good, some bad. The bad had caused him to doubt what he used to believe in so easily. The good, he could share with Ruthie and perhaps protect her from harm. But it meant spending more time with her… time that would open up his heart to more temptation and pain.

He might regret what he was about to do, but it was better than trying to merely "have faith" that Ruthie would stay safe.

"I think you should take some self-defense classes," he began.

"I don't think—"

"I'll teach the classes myself. At my office. You close early on Saturday, right?" At her nod, he continued. "Come to my office. Bring your friends." He thought of the teenage girl living in the car. "Daisy, too."

"That's very sweet of you, but—"

There was only one way to convince her, and he didn't hesitate using it. "Pop would really be disappointed if you turned this down."

Ruthie looked away and fidgeted with her pony-tail holder, buying time to consider his offer. And to consider what the enforced time together might do to the fragile threads holding them together as "family friends." Would it bring them back together, or would it create a permanent divide in their relationship?

She had thought her feelings for Gray would die after all this time apart. But now she believed even more strongly than ever that he was the only man for her. He was a good man. Kind. Strong. And protective, not only of her but of her friends. What woman wouldn't want a man like that?

The only two things standing between them were her belief and whatever had caused him to stop trusting in God. He saw her faith as the problem that had pushed them apart. But Ruthie suddenly saw it as the solution that could bring them back together.

Last night while reading her Bible before bed, a message had planted itself in her mind, promising her hope and a future. At the time, she hadn't known why it had stood out for her. But now she became convinced it was a message for her to accept the opportunity to spend time with Gray.

Perhaps their spending time together during the self-defense lessons would allow him to see once again the personal values and core beliefs that had originally bonded them, first in friendship and later in love. All she had to do was take some self-defense classes with him and join him in recovering Naoko's doll. God would do the rest.

He was waiting for her answer.

Ruthie smiled and stuck out her hand. "It's a deal," she said as he closed his fingers around hers. She couldn't prevent a joyful smile at the rightness of his touch. "We have a lot to learn. Don't we?"

Chapter Four

The next night, Ruthie arrived at Sobo's hospital room just as Gray was leaving. He wore slacks and a jacket, an indicator he had just come from work. Shadows hung under his dark eyes, a telltale sign that his desire to protect this loved one was just out of his reach. He nodded toward the visitor area at the end of the hall, where they could talk without disturbing his grandmother.

She followed him and settled onto one of the two scuffed blue chairs in a tiny nook outfitted with a table, a lamp, and a few books and magazines apparently left there by previous visitors. He took the seat opposite her and smoothed his slacks. Without ado, she blurted the question that she feared to ask. "How is Sobo?"

He shook his head. "Not better, not worse. There's a lot of pain in her leg, but she's trying not to show it. Just keeps asking to go home."

"That's a Bristow for you. Stoic all the way." It concerned Ruthie that Sobo wasn't improving. She wished things were different between Gray and her so they could pray together. Instead, she offered up a quick silent request for God to watch over Sobo and speed her healing.

"Any luck with those phone calls?"

She shook her head. "I called every customer in my database, and none of them had purchased the doll." The good news was that many took the call as a nudge to come back to the shop. As much as she appreciated the business, she would much rather have found Sobo's doll.

He reached into his pocket, pulled out a sheet of paper on which a photo of their parking area had been printed and handed it to her. "The guitar shop across the street captured this image on their security camera." He jabbed a finger at a small older-model foreign car. "That is most likely the car that your mystery shopper drove."

Ruthie moved the light under the lamp and leaned in. "No one's in the car and the only person in the area is a workman climbing a ladder in front of the bookstore to wash windows." She squinted and looked closer. "And it's impossible to see the make and model of the car, much less the license number."

"Exactly, which is why you should have your own security camera. If this were taken from the vantage point of the Abundance shops, we could have gotten a clear picture."

Coulda, shoulda, woulda was what her mother used to say whenever anyone focused on might-have-beens. Although her mother had suffered some hardships, first raising a young daughter by herself, then marrying a man who turned out to be nothing like the charmer he'd initially presented himself as, Ellen had maintained a cheerful attitude of love and hope. Even when money was tight, steering her to work in a factory job that ultimately claimed her life, she had encouraged Ruthie to focus on what was possible and go after the blessings God had in store for her. Ruthie had taken her mother's lessons to heart as a young girl and had mostly managed to avoid stewing in regrets and wishful thinking. Until Gray, that is.

"I'll do something about security at the shop. I promise." Although her promise came out sounding slightly testy, she really did appreciate his concern for her safety. "When you talked to people at the neighboring businesses, did anyone mention having seen an elegant-looking Asian lady?"

His lip twitched in a tell that revealed he had something more to share. Ruthie tried not to focus on his lips. Just looking at his firm mouth made her think of the kissing dolls…and of all the kissing the dolls had witnessed.

"We're in luck," he said, rubbing his hands together. "Sort of."

Her heart did a mini surge then plummet. Not so much because of the addendum to his first statement but because there once had been a day when he hadn't believed in luck. If something good had happened, he would have attributed it to "divine providence" or an "unexpected blessing." Rather than acknowledge luck, Ruthie preferred to believe that God was in control and, therefore, deserved the credit.

"The classic-car guy happened to see the car pull into the parking area and was like a bee on nectar."

Ruthie's hopes soared. "Did he see the woman? Better yet, does he know who she is?"

"Not up close, but he told me the car is a 1961 Mazda Coupe. He drooled over it while the woman went inside to shop."

She blinked, trying to understand how that information could possibly bring them closer to the owner of the car. And closer to Sobo's doll.

"Now that we know what kind of car it is," he said, connecting the dots for her, "we can call local antique automobile clubs and ask if they have a member with that make and model. And if so, we'll just ask them to put us in touch with the owner."

Okay, that made sense. Gray offered to make the calls, for which she was grateful, and promised to let her know when any information turned up.

"Thank you," she said, and wished she could snap her fingers and clear away the mystery of where the doll might be. Just as she wished she could clear away the cloud of confusion that had settled over Gray's heart four years ago. And while she was snapping her fingers, it would be nice to clear away the distance that had come between them.

Their briefing over, they stood together. After making arrangements for their first self-defense lesson tomorrow, they said their goodbyes. As naturally as they had done a thousand times before, Gray leaned in to her—close enough for her to smell the unique, warm scent of his cologne. Close enough to resurrect dreams she had no business dreaming.

And then, just as suddenly, he apparently remembered the Dear Jane letter and the four years that stood between them and stopped himself, leaving Ruthie yearning for the goodbye hug and kiss that never came.

* * *

Pop met her at the door to Sobo's room. The worried frown that crossed his features indicated he must have seen the unsettled emotions that still swirled around her, but he kept his thoughts to himself. Ruthie knew that nothing he could say would help anyway.

He put his arm around her. Grateful that one of the Bristow men was still willing to hug her, she snuggled into the kindly embrace. His gray-stubbled cheek scratched against her temple.

"You okay?" he asked.

Of course she wasn't. It seemed that every encounter with Gray was an opportunity for him to reject her again. The optimistic side of her clung to the possibility of their getting back together. Even so, she wondered how many times he'd have to push her away before she gave up the notion of their becoming a couple again. At first she'd been excited about the possibility of spending more time in Gray's company, excited that God seemed to be using their search for the doll as a means to bring them together, but now she wondered if the negatives would outweigh the positives. Even so, she still believed that God meant for her and Gray to be together. She still clung to the verse that promised God had "plans to give you hope and a future." On days like this, hope seemed mighty thin while she waited for the future.

Her heart-adopted grandfather already had one woman to worry about, so she wasn't about to add her comparatively small frets to his concerns. Besides, Sobo was the number-one priority right now. "Sure. I'm good."

He looked as though he didn't believe it.

Lowering his voice, he said, "Let's not mention the doll yet. Naoko needs to concentrate on healing right now, and I don't want any bad news to set her back."

"Of course." She gave him a brief recap of her conversation with Gray and tried to sound more optimistic than she felt about the possibility of the doll's reappearance.

Ruthie entered the small private hospital room, Pop on her heels. The tiny woman looked even smaller than usual, with white sheets and blankets covering all but her red, swollen left leg and one shoulder that revealed part of a not-so-fashionable cotton gown that tied at the neck. She wore no makeup, and the lack of her trademark dark eyeliner made her look unusually pale. On seeing Ruthie enter the room, Sobo started to pull the blanket over her leg, then seemed to think better of it. She covered it with the sheet instead. Pop had mentioned that her leg was painful, so Ruthie assumed that even the light weight of the blanket must have been too much.

Ruthie eased herself onto the bed, taking care not to jostle it, and sat just as Sobo had done when she, as a teen, had been in bed with the flu and again after wisdom-tooth extractions. She took the hand of her honorary grandmother and held it between her own. The usual pale pink nail polish had been scrubbed clean, and the fingers that had once seemed so strong and sure now felt thin and frail.

Sobo pursed her lips. "If you eat this hospital food," she said with a sweep of her free hand toward the barely touched dinner tray, "you have no appetite."

To take their minds off the frustrations of hospital confinement, Ruthie chatted about the happenings at

Abundance: Savannah's latest alterations to the wedding dress she'd been tinkering with since her teens, Paisley's successful experiment with smoked-salmon-and-sour-cream finger sandwiches, and her own acquisition of an antique iron grate that she planned to repurpose into a decorative end table. She steered clear of any mention of the dark-haired man who had graced her shop with his presence nearly every day this week.

Sobo lifted her head. "That's good. Very good. You sell the barley table? And *ranzatsu?*"

Well, she'd taken the other woman's mind off of hospital troubles, but now her own thoughts had been steered back to the one who'd taken home the barley table and the memories they'd shared over it.

"Yes, the table went to a good home where it will sit in the new owner's kitchen." She hurried on before Sobo could question her further. "Your hats have been a big hit. Several will be worn in the Monument Avenue Easter parade later this month, and a couple of ladies are planning to wear them to church."

"Gray's sister played with them when she was little. Catie stood in front of mirror and put hand on her hip." Sobo's expression softened and she appeared to drift down memory lane. "Big brother Gray snatched it off her head and ran through the house. He say she squeal like a pig. But he give it back," she added, quick to redeem her grandson's reputation as the protector everyone knew him to be.

Ruthie sighed. Just as he had taken the hat from his sister, he had snatched her heart right out of her chest. Then, in an apparent act of honor, he had tried to give it back. As far as she was concerned, he still owned it.

From the vinyl chair in the corner of the room, Pop

clicked the remote and switched the channel away from the celebrity-gossip program it had been on. She wished it were as easy to switch the subject with Sobo. The channel landed on a game show, which immediately switched to a commercial urging viewers to watch the eleven-o'clock evening news to find out more about the prowler that had been spotted in the Museum District the previous evening. He zapped the channel again, but not soon enough.

Sobo pointed to the TV screen. "I already heard about that man," she informed her husband. She squeezed Ruthie's hand in a grip that was much stronger than expected for a woman who was so ill. "You and the girls lock your doors. Don't come out at night, no matter what."

"I will," she promised, not bothering to mention that she and her roommates already took plenty of precautions. After what Paisley had been through as a teen in an unsupervised situation with a boy she had unwisely trusted, her roommate was relentless about urging the rest of them never to take chances with their safety. "And Gray is going to teach the Abundance gals and me some personal safety and self-defense tips tomorrow."

Rather than calming Sobo as planned, the last statement seemed to trouble her.

"Sunday is for going to church. You do safety tips another day."

"Tomorrow is Saturday, Sobo."

Pop leaned forward in his chair.

Sobo pulled her hand from Ruthie's and pushed it through her mussed hair. "No. Is Sunday."

Now Pop rose from the chair and moved to the bed,

where he carefully placed his big palm on his wife's forehead. "Not running a fever. Do you know what year this is?"

"Of course I do." Sobo squinted at him as if he was the one with the problem, not she. But to appease him, she named the year, month and calendar date but was off by one day.

Worry filled Pop's eyes. He was overreacting, but the pair had been together for many years, and Ruthie knew him to be as protective as—if not more protective than—Gray.

"When you're in the hospital, time blurs," Ruthie assured him. "There are no laundry days, grocery days or gardening days to keep track of the passing time."

Sobo nodded. "It's all the time poke me, give me pills and make me eat bad food. All same-same, every day."

Pop accepted what they said, but it didn't seem to calm his nerves much to hear that her temporary memory lapse was normal. He paced a bit, then moved toward the door. "I'm going to get some coffee," he said. "Do either of you want anything?"

At their negative replies, he abruptly left the room.

"He's worried about you," Ruthie said, stating the obvious.

"I know. He's a good man." Sobo drew her gaze away from the door and fixed her brown eyes on Ruthie, who took the chair he had vacated. "He all the time looks out for me, looks out for his children and his grandchildren. Gray is just like him. He takes care of people. Even when he was a little boy."

Ruthie knew about his protective nature and how it had been shaped by his father's military service.

Sometimes he'd taken his assigned duty a little too seriously, according to Catie, who had complained the time he interrogated her date and intimidated the teen so that he never asked her out again. Although Gray's little sister had been annoyed at the time, she later confessed to Ruthie that it had been for the best, since the guy had gone out with her best friend and turned out to be a jerk.

"All the Bristows served in army," Sobo continued. "Gray fight in Afghanistan. Father fight in Desert Storm. And grandfather fight in Korea."

Ruthie cleared her throat. "Is that how you met Pop? When he went to Korea?" He'd never talked much about his time over there, and other than a short study of the war in a history class, Ruthie knew little about what he must have experienced. The episodes of *M.A.S.H.* reruns she'd watched on television gave her the impression Pop must have gone to Tokyo for the occasional weekend leave, but since neither of them had ever answered her questions, she was left to imagine a delightfully romantic love-at-first-sight kind of meeting.

Sobo looked away, leaving Ruthie to continue imagining how the pair came to be together. "War changed Gray." She lightly touched two fingers to her swollen leg, letting Ruthie know the pain remained. "He's not the same now. To you. To us."

Ruthie didn't want to talk about this. Didn't want to be reminded of all she'd lost. Of the eager, energetic man who'd left to do his duty and returned with the light in his eyes now hidden behind dark memories that he refused to share.

Sobo must have noticed Ruthie's concern. "He will

be back. He will find peace again. He will look at you and smile." The elderly woman leaned on her elbows and pushed herself up in bed, as if she would muscle her way through her grandson's difficulty just as she was trying to muscle her way through her own physical recovery. "I know, because I pray. I pray you will someday be my granddaughter-by-law."

Ruthie's heart tightened at the familiar misspeak of the term *granddaughter-in-law.* When she had come to live with the Bristows, they had immediately started referring to her as their honorary granddaughter. Soon after she and Gray had become engaged, Sobo delightfully claimed her as a "granddaughter by love," an affectionate acknowledgment that even though she and Gray weren't yet legally joined, her union in the family was officially sealed by love.

"God listens to prayers," Sobo said. "And He will answer."

Ruthie had no doubt about that. She just wished she knew when and what the answer might be.

Chapter Five

Gray was still pushing furniture out of the way in the reception area when Ruthie propped her bicycle in the common hallway and opened the door to his suite of offices. He took a deep breath and reminded himself to focus on the goal for the next couple of hours…to teach Ruthie and her friends self-protection, all the while trying to protect his heart from her. Or, more important, keep her at a safe arm's length.

He kept his eyes on the chairs that he pushed against the wall, but his peripheral vision traitorously afforded him a view of her removing her bicycle helmet, releasing her reddish-brown hair to tumble to her slim shoulders. She popped a pair of white earbuds out of her ears, tucked them into the helmet and set everything on a table near the door. Then she turned slowly in place, apparently taking in the size of the room, the decor, its sole other inhabitant…whatever it is women do when they size up a place.

Why had he invited her here? Why had he opened the door to his inner sanctum? He turned his back to her and shoved the coffee table against the wall.

Maybe if he pretended she wasn't there, she'd disappear. Better yet, maybe the urge to take her in his arms and kiss away four lonely years would disappear. Sure, he'd broken up with her and dated other people, as he was certain she must have done, but he'd always subconsciously compared them to Ruthie. No matter how nice or pretty or nonreligious those women were, they never quite measured up to the standard set by his first real love.

Human will was only so strong, and he turned toward the woman who'd been a source of pleasure and pain over the years.

"Nice lair." She bent and removed a rubber band from the ankle of her yoga pants.

Okay, he was only human. He gave her his full attention, then wished he hadn't. She hadn't changed much since she had first come to live with his grandparents. Still slim, but now more womanly in her appearance, she moved in quick and easy—even cheerful—movements. To his immense regret, she still made him want to take her under his arm and protect her from the sources of all pain in the world, including himself.

He cleared the knot of tension from his throat. "Where are the others?"

Ruthie straightened and caught him watching her, but did not blush as she might have in the past. She just seemed both pleased and matter-of-fact, as if his attention was a foregone conclusion. It was the same confidence he'd seen in her whenever she prayed for something and then received the result she'd asked for.

"They went to pick up Daisy. I had to finish some work at the shop, so I told them to go ahead and I would meet them here. They should arrive soon." She smiled and swept her glance around the room once more. "You must be doing well to have such a nice office. I'm glad for you."

On the one hand, he was glad they had this time to themselves. On the other, he wished the others would hurry and get here so their presence could dilute the thick tension in the room.

"It's not all mine," he said. "I share the receptionist, meeting rooms and storage area with a lawyer." He didn't bother to mention that he was already outgrowing the space and would need to look elsewhere when the lease expired. "Come on. I'll give you a quick tour while we wait for the others to show up."

It shouldn't have mattered, but he wanted to impress her. Wanted to know she approved of all he had achieved. Of all he had become.

He stopped himself on that last one. She might approve of the signs of business success he showed her, but if he himself didn't approve of the kind of man he had become, how could she? He shook off the uneasy feeling and steered the conversation to something he was only slightly more comfortable talking about.

"I called the antique-car clubs in Richmond and even spread out to all the ones I could find in Virginia."

She'd been casing the perimeter of his office, trailing a finger over the books in the case, lingering especially over one title. *Security Management: How to Identify Vulnerabilities*. She looked back at him and smiled, a hint of knowing tugging at her lips.

"Unfortunately, none of their members has a '61 Mazda Coupe."

Ruthie frowned, but even that didn't dim the prettiness of her features. Didn't make him want to kiss her any less. She moved to the window and glanced down at the street. Then she dropped her hand to the framed photograph on the sill.

"But one club was aware of the car." *Good! Look away from the photo.* "Said they'd seen it on West Franklin Street, near the Maury monument."

She nodded and turned her attention back to the picture. "Maybe we can drive around and look to see if it's parked on the street. Then knock on the neighboring doors until we find the owner and ask to buy the doll back."

"I hate to burst your bubble, but a car like that is not likely to be parked on the street. It's probably in a garage." And right now he wished that picture were hidden away in that garage.

He moved closer to take it from her hands but got distracted by the wispy waves of her hair.

"I've always loved this picture," she said, holding it up for him to see. "Sobo and Pop were so happy to have the entire family together."

They were happy because their whole brood had been gathered together at the same time, a near impossibility given his father's and uncle's crazy work schedules at that time. He and his sister, their parents and his aunt and uncle and their three kids all smiled at the camera. And, of course, Ruthie. Her smile was the biggest. And prettiest. The photo was taken about a year after she had come to live with his grandparents. Shortly before their first date. Sobo had arranged everyone on the broad front-porch steps, then enlisted a passerby to seal the image of all of them in a photograph. He and Ruthie had stood on opposite sides of the stairs, but the camera's flash had caught the glimmer of awareness toward each other in their eyes.

He reached for the photo and set it back in its place on the windowsill, hoping to end this conversation before she gave too much thought to why he'd chosen to display this particular picture. "The others should be getting here soo—"

"Oh, look, they just drove up." Ruthie spun away from the window to launch herself across the room but smacked into his chest instead.

He grabbed her arms, righted her and summoned his military training to try to calm the rapid pounding of his heart. She looked as nervous as he felt, and he wondered if she was reacting to him or to the fact that her friends would be left standing on the front stoop if they didn't get out there soon and unlock the front door. A twinge of pride made him wish for the former, but common sense dictated it would be better for both of them if she hadn't been foolish enough to let her heart stay stuck in the past.

Foolish like him.

He set his jaw and stepped away from the window—away from the woman at the window—and marched back to the reception area to let in the four laughing women, all but one dressed in exercise clothes. Daisy wore jeans.

He could feel Ruthie's presence behind him as he directed the latecomers inside.

"What?" Savannah's gaze shot past him to Ruthie. "Did we interrupt something?"

It was anyone's guess what she must have seen on Ruthie's face, but he decided now would be a good time to direct their attention to the purpose of this gathering. "We were just waiting for everyone to arrive so we could get started."

Even to his own ears, his words sounded gruff and unwelcoming. Daisy widened her eyes and took two tentative steps back, letting the others serve as her buffer. Great. Now he'd gone and intimidated the kid.

Paisley, on the other hand, was not the least bit put out by his tone. She waltzed over to the chairs lined up around the wall and flung her purse onto one of them. "We invited ourselves over to Nikki's for a movie and sleepover tonight," she announced. "Ruthie, there's an extra sleeping bag for you. We're going to watch *Casablanca* because Daisy has never seen it. Do you two want to join us for the movie?"

He answered quickly. Maybe a little too quickly. "No!"

Ruthie's voice blended with his, but she was polite enough to add a thank-you after her no and explained that she had paperwork to finish.

The last thing he needed was to watch a romantic movie with her in the same room and all her friends shooting speculative glances at them. All he wanted to do was find Sobo's doll, give Ruthie some personal-safety skills and keep a polite distance from her at family gatherings.

He needed to get rolling with this self-defense lesson. The sooner they got started, the sooner it would end. And then they could go back to living their mostly separate lives.

He moved to the door, pushed it closed and turned the lock.

Ruthie moved to the middle of the floor, behind Savannah, Paisley and Nikki. She stood in the back row with Daisy, and they exchanged encouraging glances. Each wanted something from Gray. Daisy wanted to learn how to make it safely on the street until she was able to get her and her father into some decent housing. And if affordable precluded decent, she'd need the skills in her future home, as well. Ruthie just wanted Gray's love. For herself and for the God he used to know.

She gave herself a mental kick for allowing herself to jump back on that train of thought. Sure, he had that picture of her—of the whole family, actually, but she was quite visible in it—on his windowsill. That didn't necessarily mean anything. Not by itself, it didn't. But paired with his noticeable agitation when she had picked it up, she'd venture a guess that he still harbored a minuscule ember, maybe even a tiny flame, for her.

Even so, she reminded herself, if God wanted them together—and she believed He did—He would allow it to happen. In the meantime, she would be wise not to rush God's timing. Instead, she would accept opportunities such as this self-defense class to spend time with Gray while God worked on softening his heart. Not to mention using proximity and that fragrance he used to like to snag his full attention.

She tried to pay attention while Gray went over the handouts. She mentally mapped out the route by which she sometimes rode her bicycle to work and contemplated whether she should detour around a particular shady block with the spooky overhanging tree limbs and unkempt yards. Considered the height of the bushes in front of their house and wondered if they were tall enough and thick enough to hide an aggressor. And decided she *should* get a pepper-spray keychain for those rare occasions when she opened or closed the shops by herself.

By now Gray had finished going over the written materials and moved on to the block, evade and escape demonstrations. "I'll be the attacker. Who wants to go first?"

The front row moved back as one, putting Ruthie and Daisy at point.

Gray stared for a long moment at Ruthie, and she thought for sure he was going to pull her out to the middle of the floor. Her heart fluttered crazily at the thought of him wrapping his arms around her in a mock capture, and she doubted her body would obey when she told it to block, evade and escape his warm, strong clutches.

He jerked his gaze away from her, leading her to wonder if he'd somehow read her mind. Maybe he worried she would attack *him*.

"You," he said, pointing to Daisy. "Let's show 'em how it's done."

The teen hesitated and looked to Ruthie for guidance. Daisy wasn't normally a timid girl, but in this case, Gray's large size and drill-sergeant demeanor seemed to overwhelm her. Considering his earlier lapse in Southern hospitality, it was no wonder the girl found him overpowering.

Gray eased back, apparently having come to the same conclusion. Bypassing Ruthie, he beckoned Paisley, the smallest of the five females, to step forward. "You two will be partners." A smart move, considering Daisy's uncharacteristic show of nervousness.

The circle widened, and he coached the pair through

the exercise. "Paisley, you'll be the attacker, so come right here behind Daisy and—"

"I'd rather not." Paisley backed away, palms out. Her fingers trembled ever so slightly.

Gray scowled, obviously trying to get his head around her reluctance to play the role, then softened. "Okay, you'll be the victim. Just stand here and—"

Paisley shook her head and sidestepped his guiding hand. She looked to Savannah, concern marring her delicate features. "Perhaps I shouldn't have come. This was a mistake."

"Come on. It'll be fine," Savannah urged. "We all need this training." She stressed the word *all* as if to remind Paisley that she needed it even more than the others.

Now Gray was confused. And Ruthie was almost as in the dark as he was about why her friend had developed a sudden reluctance to participate in learning the techniques they'd come here for. All she knew was that something had happened in Paisley's past, before she came as a young college student to the U.S. Something she didn't talk about.

Gray rubbed the palm of his hand over his jaw while he seemed to ponder how to handle this unexpected resistance. "It's hard to teach a hands-on demonstration without going hands-on," he said at last.

Savannah stepped forward to take Paisley's place and shooed her friend to join the other observers. "She has her reasons. Show me what to do."

With Paisley watching from the sidelines, Gray showed them how to walk and scan their surroundings for potential predators in a way that exuded confidence rather than fear. By the time the one-man demonstration ended, Paisley seemed to have gotten over her aversion to the exercise, and she and Nikki paired up to practice with each other. Then Savannah and Daisy chose each other as partners, leaving Ruthie to act out the scenario with Gray.

Was it her imagination, or did his Adam's apple bob when he realized he'd be paired with her? Ruthie involuntarily mimicked the action, swallowed hard and, following his instruction, aimed the heel of her left hand toward his nose.

Gray intercepted her slow-motion gesture, fully aware that she was afraid of hurting him. He grabbed her arm firmly and pulled her to him, coaching her through the countermoves to block his advances. If only it were this easy to teach her to block the furtive looks he often found himself aiming her way. But every time he caught her gaze, her wide hazel eyes projected the message that he had already knocked her off her feet, without even touching her.

He still cared about her. Couldn't be close like this without caring. And wanting to kiss her. It was clear something was going to give, and he was afraid it would be his determination to do right by Ruthie and hold her at arm's length.

It was getting late. He'd better end this class before he did something stupid. Like pull her into his arms and give her a kiss that would make her forget her own name. If he did that, though, he'd better be prepared to forget about the reason they no longer shared the same faith.

Her faith involved reliance on a capricious God who sometimes answered prayers and other times left a believer floundering alone and wondering why he had been abandoned. His faith, on the other hand, involved reliance on knowledge, strength and sometimes a bit of luck. Those were what had gotten him through the tough times…the times when God hadn't been there for him.

"Before we wrap it up," he said, "look around you for a weapon to swing or throw at the assailant and an exit route for escape. No matter what your environment, always make yourself aware of the tools at hand that can assist you if you're ever approached by someone intent on harming you. Even if you don't render your attacker unconscious, you'll want to throw him off-balance to give you a few seconds to get away."

Ruthie didn't need to throw a table lamp at him. She had already knocked him off kilter just by being here. Just by being herself. By being the same woman he'd fallen in love with. Worse…by having grown into an even better version of the young woman whose heart he'd been forced to break a few years ago.

After they restored the reception area to order, the young women left amid a flurry of thank-yous and see-you-laters. All but Ruthie, who had put on her bike helmet and now poked the white earbuds back into her ears.

Gray reached forward and plucked them out. He wrapped the cord around his hand, tied a tidy little knot and handed the earphones back to her. "How are you going to be aware of your surroundings with music pounding in your ears?"

She pushed them into a tiny key pocket in her yoga pants. "Oops, forgot."

Outside, Savannah's car pulled away from the curb, drawing his attention to the fading daylight. Ruthie's bike ride wouldn't take more than about fifteen or twenty minutes, but he didn't like the idea of her going home to an empty house at dusk.

He pulled his keys from his pocket. "You can take off your helmet. I'll give you a ride home."

"That's not necessary. I'm fine."

Of course she was fine. Better than fine. She was superb, a fact that wouldn't go unnoticed by someone with criminal intent. Sure, the likelihood of her being accosted by some random stranger was slim, but recent news reports of a prowler in the area had sent his protective instincts into overdrive.

"Okay, you go first," he said, holding the door. "I'll follow you in my car to make sure you get home safely."

She did a cute little eye roll reminiscent of her teen years when Sobo had insisted she let him walk with her whenever she left the house after dark.

"Bristow men protect their *gokazoku*," Sobo had said, referring to family. "And their women let them."

Ruthie hesitated, then a tiny glimmer lit her eyes. A glimmer that he had come to know meant she was up to something. A glimmer that had him wondering if he was about to be laid low by this little snip of a woman.

"I suppose we are still *kazoku*," she said, using the more intimate version of the word for family. She swept the helmet off her head and sent those red strands flying. She stepped past him into the hallway where her bike awaited. "Thank you. Are you sure you have room in your car?"

He had plenty of room in the car for her bike. But nowhere near enough for all the baggage they lugged between them.

* * *

Ruthie's spirits soared on the drive home. There was still hope.

She'd noticed the awareness that had passed between them, as she was sure he'd also noticed. Yet here he was, driving her home despite everything that had transpired between them, both today and in the past. She was still *kazoku* to him. Not sister family but bonded-by-the-heart family. Once he let someone in, that person was always his.

Gray pulled into an open parking spot in front of her house on Floyd Avenue. Shadows fell beneath the ancient maple tree, casting the sidewalk in a mottled pattern that created an illusion of movement beneath her feet. The house lay dark before her. Ordinarily, she wouldn't think twice about the eerie effect, but today's class had made her hyperaware of all aspects of her surroundings. Especially of the big strong male hoisting her bike out of his car.

She moved ahead, keys in hand, and pushed the gate open on her side of the house. Divided down the middle, with separate entrances and a white picket fence between the two halves, the blue two-story frame house exuded a quaint charm that harkened back to the early 1920s.

Should she invite Gray in? How would he interpret such an invitation? Would it scare him off? Despite a few bumpy moments, the day had gone well, and the last thing she wanted was to make things awkward between them.

Something snapped. At first Ruthie thought the noise came from the latch she lifted to open the gate. She moved it again, up and down, but the noise did not repeat itself. Their neighbors, a young married couple with a spoiled miniature dachshund, were away for the weekend, so the sound couldn't be attributed to Rotten Ralphie snuffling through the postage-stamp yard.

A cool breeze swept over her, raising gooseflesh under her jacket sleeves. Now she peered through dim light into the neighboring yard but saw nothing that warranted alarm. She gave herself a mental shake for being so silly and reminded herself that a combat-trained former soldier followed just a few yards behind her. The sound had probably come from the neighbor two doors down who liked to cook out on the barbecue all year long.

She pushed through the gate, Gray bringing up the rear, and this time something rustled sharply on the other side of the divider fence. She spun toward the sound to glimpse a quick movement in the next yard.

Her heart lurched into her throat, and she clenched the keys so hard they would certainly leave imprints on her skin. A nondescript brown dog nosed along the bushes, its tail curved upward like a feathery plume. Just as quickly as she had started at the sound, she blew out a relieved breath and proceeded up the steps to the front door.

She pushed the key into the lock. Every now and then an occasional stray animal wandered the neighborhood, but she had no idea how this one had managed to find its way inside the fence. She'd check it after Gray brought the bike in to see if it wore a collar and tags.

Behind her the bike suddenly clattered to the ground, and feet pounded up the paved walkway. She turned just in time to see Gray vault sideways over the waist-high divider fence, his movements as fluid as a gymnast's.

The bush shook violently in front of the latticework, and a man in camouflage clothing bolted from his hiding place in the neighbor's yard. Gray burst after him and rounded the yard in pursuit, the brown dog hot on his heels.

"Go inside and lock the door," he ordered, then disappeared around the side of the house.

Ruthie stood frozen for what seemed like minutes but was probably only a couple of seconds before she collected herself enough to reach for her cell phone and dial 911. She quickly gave the dispatcher her address and a summary of what had happened.

"Does the man have a gun?" asked the woman at the other end of the line. "Or a weapon of any kind?"

A gun? It hadn't occurred to her that Gray might be chasing an armed man. He might be good at self-defense, but bullets were stronger. And even if the stranger wasn't armed, his dog had teeth that it might be willing to use to protect its owner.

"I don't know," she said. "He had a medium-size dog with him, but I don't know if it's aggressive."

After shakily answering a few more questions, she disconnected the phone and begged God to watch over the man who was willing to protect her, even at risk of harm to himself.

High-pitched yelps resounded from the back of the house. Ruthie's chest squeezed so that she could barely breathe. Remembering Gray's admonition to always be aware of potential weapons, she scanned the front porch and grabbed a ceramic pot filled with soil…the intended home for Savannah's future begonias.

By now footsteps trod slowly and unevenly on the flagstone path that led from the backyard. She doubted the prowler would be daring enough to make his way back here, but an equally disturbing thought occurred to her. What if Gray had been injured and was now limping back?

She had prayed for him throughout his tour of duty in Afghanistan, even after their breakup, and he had returned home safe and uninjured. One hand automatically curled, her thumb touching her fingers. *Please, God, You kept him safe before. Don't let anything happen to him now.*

Ruthie sprinted back toward the gate, the pot of dirt tucked under her arm, leaped over the prone bicycle and flung open the gate to her neighbor's yard. With an extra burst of adrenaline, she lifted the pot in preparation for defense, skirted the yard and slammed to a halt.

In the shadows of the narrow corridor between this house and the neighbor's, the tall male figure loomed before her. He clutched something in his arms and moved toward her.

"I told you to go inside," Gray said, his tone abrupt but tinged with concern and maybe a little fear. For her?

"I was…" She set the begonia pot on the ground. Was he all right? Was that a limp?

As he trudged closer, thin rays from the streetlights fell on him, and she was able to discern the brown dog that he held close to his chest. The dog lifted its head and tentatively licked Gray's chin. Another female fallen prey to his strength and charm.

"You were praying, weren't you?" he said with a

nod toward her left hand. The question sounded accusatory. Almost angry.

She looked down at her hand, knowing even before seeing it that the familiar gesture had tipped him off to what she'd been doing. He used to tease her for the way she prayed when in public. Her mother had taught her to pray with both hands folded in front of her, and that was how Ruthie preferred to talk to God. Ideally, on her knees. But sometimes, when she was driving or involved in some other activity that didn't lend itself to such a reverent posture, she liked to show her respect by pressing together the thumb and fingers of one hand. A one-handed version of folded hands. Gray had often joked that the formation resembled the head of a baby bird, and he had made shadow puppets on the wall to demonstrate. "Got your emu?" he'd asked when she tearfully kissed him goodbye the day he deployed.

He'd been joking then, but he didn't seem very amused by it now.

"Looks like your God forgot to watch out for this little one."

Chapter Six

A crimson stain covered the short brown fur on the dog's shoulder and smeared across Gray's arm. In the darkening shadows, it looked like a scene from a horror movie.

"Oh, no. What happened to her?" She quickly scanned both man and animal for further injuries, but in the dark it was hard to tell what additional damage they may have suffered. "Are you all right?"

"I'm okay. I had just grabbed the guy by the scruff of the shirt when Calamity Jane here had a close encounter with the metal corner of a lawn chair. Her squalling distracted me, and the prowler got away." Then, perhaps in an effort to reassure Ruthie, he added, "We don't know that he was up to any harm. He may have just been a Peeping Tom."

Not that it made any difference to her. Either way— prowler or Peeping Tom—it was just plain creepy to have a strange man lurking near her home.

The Lab mix lowered her ears and extended her nose as Ruthie approached. The dog sniffed her hand and gave her fingers a friendly lick. And to think she had worried this sweet dog might try to bite Gray.

"We should get her inside and see if she needs to be looked at by a vet," she said.

They walked back to her house with Gray in take-charge mode. "Get the gate." "We need to call the police." "Don't forget to let your neighbors know what's going on." "Let's wash the blood off this dog so we can see how bad she's hurt."

At any other time, she might have chafed under his bossiness, but after what had just happened, she appreciated his calm certainty about what needed to be done next.

The police arrived just as Gray had maneuvered the dog into the bathtub to get cleaned up. While Ruthie gently sprayed water over the dog's cut, Gray went to the door and gave his statement and a description of the man he had chased out of the bushes. Then they swapped places, and she told her version of what happened.

After she showed the police officers out, she went back to the bathroom, where Gray toweled off the dog, taking care to avoid rubbing the laceration on its shoulder. Gray had already washed the blood off his own arms, but the stain remained on the sleeve and front of his shirt. The scary evidence of his close encounter reminded her that it could just as easily have been Gray's blood staining his shirt. Ruthie prayed a silent prayer of thanks for God's protection during their run-in with the prowler.

"All that blood made the cut look worse than it really is," he said, pointedly ignoring her emu hand while he dabbed liquid from a brown bottle onto the wound.

"A little peroxide, some food to fatten her up and soon she'll be good as new."

Gray rose to his feet, and the dog shook herself and wandered off to the kitchen as if to say the idea of food was a good one. Ruthie rummaged through the refrigerator and filled a bowl with leftover roasted chicken, a sprinkling of peas and carrots and a small dab of mashed potatoes.

"Calamity Jane," she said, referring to Gray's earlier description of the dog. They watched the animal devour the sumptuous fare, and after it finished, she added a bit more chicken. "Jane doesn't seem to fit, but perhaps Calamity would fit…or Cali for short."

Gray shook his head. "Don't do it. If you name her, you'll end up keeping her."

He was right. If she didn't commit to the dog in the first place, it would hurt less later on when it came time to part with her. Too bad the dog had already become Cali in her mind and would remain so forever. Just as her heart still claimed Gray as her fiancé. Ruthie found it easy to make room in her heart for more loved ones. Letting go proved to be more of a challenge.

"You shouldn't stay here tonight," he said. "In case the prowler comes back."

Right again. Part of her wanted to argue that she'd be fine staying here by herself, but the truth was she'd really rather not remain in an empty house while a potentially dangerous man roamed the neighborhood. Although the guy had likely been scared off for good, there was still the slight chance he might come back for the dog or whatever else had drawn him here in the first place.

"I suppose I could go over to Nikki's place. They

already have a sleeping bag for me, and we could put down a blanket for Cali—um, the dog."

Gray reached down and rumpled the dog's ears. Cali melted under his touch and rolled over onto her back. If Ruthie had been a dog, she would have done the same thing. Instead, she tried to suppress her natural inclination to turn to putty in his presence.

"Might be a little noisy for her after what she's been through this evening," he said. "It would be quieter at Pop's house, and he could use the company."

She nodded. Pop had been spending most of his time at the hospital with Sobo, but evenings were the worst. He had admitted it was hard to climb those stairs alone and spend the night apart from his wife of almost sixty years. "Do you suppose he'd mind me bringing the dog?"

"He'd love it. Why don't you pack an overnight bag, and I'll drive you over there. We can pick up some dog food on the way."

She did as he suggested and returned a few minutes later with a duffel bag and the belt from her bathrobe to be used as a temporary leash for Cali.

"I'll bring you back here tomorrow," he promised, "and will put in a security alarm then. It's long overdue."

Ruthie's thoughts went to what Sobo had said about Sundays being reserved for going to church. If he no longer believed, did that mean the rule ceased to apply to him? "There's no need for you to work on Sunday. I'm sure a few extra days won't make any difference."

He slanted his gaze at her, making it clear he knew exactly what she was thinking. "Think of it as rescuing a lost lamb on the Sabbath. That should exempt us."

But it wasn't she who was lost and needed rescue. Silently, this time without clasping her hand, she asked God to help Gray find his way back into the fold.

Gray stood on Ruthie's front porch and rang the doorbell. The purpose of the visit was to pick up a tool he'd left here when he had installed the security system yesterday, but deep down it was really because he wanted to see her again. Four years apart had left him craving the kind of companionship that only she could offer.

No answer, so he rang the bell again. He'd called only twenty minutes ago to arrange to pick up the staple gun, so she should be here. At the very least, maybe one of her roommates was still at home since it was too early for shop hours. He couldn't be sure, but he thought he heard someone holler something from inside, so he tested the doorknob.

It turned. Annoyed that it had been left unlocked after their encounter with the prowler, he pushed the door open, leaned in and said with more than a hint of sarcasm, "It's just me, your friendly neighborhood stalker."

Ruthie's voice floated to him from the center of the narrow house. "Come on in. I left the door open for you."

He gritted his teeth. "I noticed."

As he stepped inside, he noticed an old belt and a rope dangling from a hook by the door. A leash and collar wouldn't cost much, but he knew that the mere acquisition of dog supplies would have established a sense of permanence. For that reason he'd discouraged her from buying toys and stuff for the dog, out of concern that the more financially and emotionally invested she became in the animal, the more firmly cemented it would become in her life. Although it would hurt her to give the dog up after they found out who it belonged to, he knew it would hurt her more to stand between the dog and its true owner.

Apparently the belt and rope were her temporary solution to a lack of proper equipment. He shrugged. Maybe he should pick up a decent collar and leash for Cali and give it to her with the caveat that they were to be passed along when she returned the dog.

He followed her voice to the hall and was prepared to give her a lecture for leaving the front door unlocked. But when he laid eyes on her, all such thoughts vacated his brain.

Ruthie knelt on the bathroom floor in front of the claw-foot tub, where Cali sat patiently. The dog's long ears were submissively plastered to its neck. Both woman and animal were soaking wet and covered in soapsuds, and the scent of perfumed shampoo hung heavy in the small bathroom as she made baby talk to Cali.

"You're being a good girl," she cooed. "We're almost done. Here, have a treat."

Cali's ears went up when Ruthie dug into a box of biscuits and gave her one.

Gray felt a grin steal over his face. He couldn't help it. It was an involuntary reflex when it came to Ruthie. She had a way of making people lean in to take in whatever she happened to be saying.

She babbled something about going to the vet but assured the dog in that same singsong tone that there was nothing to worry about.

"The vet? What happened?"

Although Cali had turned toward him when he had stepped into the open doorway, it wasn't until she heard his voice that she seemed to remember who he was. She reared up in the tub and offered an excited howl of greeting. Amid the commotion, she sloshed water over the side and soaked Ruthie with bathwater.

"Easy, girl." Gray hurried to Ruthie's side to help contain the dog—and the water—in the bathtub. Unfortunately, his approach only excited Cali even more, and she tried to clamber out of the tub to lick his face.

"You seem to have that effect on a lot of females," Ruthie said.

Amazingly, he managed to avoid the spray of water, but a small tidal wave, stirred by the dog's wild movements, rocked through the tub and cascaded again over Ruthie. Her red hair, which had previously been piled in a messy knot on top of her head, now clung in spiderlike strands to her face. And the pale blue T-shirt whose sleeves she had carefully folded up to keep them dry now dripped water to the tile floor. Didn't matter. To him she still looked pretty. Beautiful, in fact.

He handed her a towel and she attempted to blot herself dry, but it didn't do much good.

"I need to take her to the vet," Ruthie said, picking up their conversation where they'd left off before Cali had decided to douse her, "because she seems to be favoring the shoulder that got cut. It may be infected."

Cali bounced in the tub, clearly unaffected by the injury.

"She looks fine to me."

Ruthie blushed, her reaction telling him more clearly than words that she had gone into nurturing mode.

He hoped she wouldn't be devastated when the time came to give the dog back to its owner, but he knew the possibility was slim that she'd give Cali up without at least a few tears.

"I thought that while we're there, we'll have her scanned for a microchip, or at least see if anyone there recognizes her."

A roundabout way of saying she was emotionally adopting the dog.

She stood and pulled the rubber stopper from the bathtub drain.

"Um, you might want to change before you go." He averted his gaze and busied himself with hanging onto Cali to keep her from jumping out of the tub and soaking either of them any more than she already had.

Prompted by his suggestion, Ruthie glanced down at her shirt, blushed and pressed the sodden towel to her front.

To his credit, he fixed his eyes firmly on the dog. A real feat, considering he was 100 percent male.

"Just for that," she said, a teasing lilt in her voice, "you can finish the dog."

Then she swished—or rather, squished—out of the bathroom.

Gray's laughter followed her out the door and down the hall to her bedroom.

She changed into clean jeans and another long-sleeved T-shirt, this one black with a scalloped neckline.

His voice drifted to her again while she slipped off her sodden slippers and stepped into a pair of dry shoes. She tilted her head to hear him and picked up only broken snatches of what he was saying. "…pretty girl…so funny." And most heart catching, "…love you."

Was he talking to her? No, he couldn't be.

Cali made squealing grunts of happiness, and that was when it sank in that Gray was talking to the dog, not to her. She imagined she'd make similar noises—in her mind if not out loud—if he made a fuss over her like that. But they were still new at being back together, as friends even if not romantically. They were still on unsteady ground. With God's blessing, perhaps their relationship would grow to the point where they were comfortable enough to easily share such sentiments again.

"Okay, okay, I love you, too. Stop the kisses already." Gray's voice became muffled, as if he was covering his face to block the doggy affection. "*Blech!* Aw, come on. Knock it off."

Ruthie paused, her hand on the bedroom door's vintage glass knob. He hadn't said he loved her since that fateful letter when he'd tried to soften the blow of their breakup. The thought saddened her for a moment, but then she immediately cheered up again. He'd kissed her before, and she had faith he would kiss her again. And she was sure the kisses they'd shared were better than the sloppy doggy kisses Cali doled out.

The "I love yous" would come in good time. In God's time.

She went back to the bathroom, looking and feeling more refreshed than when she'd left.

Gray looked up at her as she entered, a smile of appreciation covering his face. It felt good to see his uncensored reaction to her…a reaction that reminded her of their better days together.

Cali, now toweled off and energized by the bath, charged past her into the front room, where she ran in crazy circles and rubbed her back against the couch. Then the little speedster threw herself onto the rug and crept, army-style, across the floor.

Gray had followed them to the front room and stood at Ruthie's side to watch Cali's antics. He laughed, the sound a bit sardonic. "This dog is living a better life than some people I've seen."

Noting the seriousness in his tone, she turned to face him. "What do you mean?"

He shook his head and walked her to the front door where he picked up the rope off the hook. "Never mind. I shouldn't have brought it up."

Cali, apparently noticing the leash in his hand, went charging to him. She attempted to sit—another clue that the dog wasn't merely a stray and had received some training—but she wiggled too much for him to get a firm grip. Gray turned away from Ruthie and focused on attaching dog to makeshift leash. At least, that was what it was supposed to look like. She had a feeling it was more of an avoidance tactic.

She put a hand on his arm. "Whatever it is, you can share everything with me."

He shook his head. "You don't want me to share everything." At that he opened the door, and Cali, already hyped up and ready to go, charged out onto the porch, pulling him after her.

The conversation conveniently ended, Ruthie was left behind to lock the door. How, she wondered, would they ever get to the root of the problem that broke them apart if they didn't share what was bothering them?

* * *

They stood on the grassy area beside Dr. Werther's office, waiting for Cali to finish sniffing and claim a spot.

"Why are you here? You didn't have to come," Ruthie told Gray. "I feel bad that you're taking time off from work for a simple checkup."

He shrugged. "Don't worry about that. I had blocked out the day to install the alarm system on your shop. I'll just get a slightly later start on it than planned."

Her question went unanswered. What *was* he doing here? Earlier he'd insisted on coming along as emotional support, but something told her there was another reason. Perhaps this was an attempt to remind her with his mere presence not to get too attached to the dog.

Too late.

Or was there a deeper reason? Did he also harbor a desire to resurrect their relationship? Was this his way of spending time with her so that any lingering sparks would have an opportunity to reignite? A tiny smile tugged at the corners of her lips.

"Your safety is my utmost concern right now," he said. "We need to find the person who was lurking around your house. If any of the staff here recognize Cali, that might lead us to the guy I chased off the other night."

Of course, his primary concern was keeping her safe. Protecting others must have been a trait that was genetically bred into his DNA.

As for Cali, it hadn't occurred to her that the dog might belong to the prowler. She had just assumed their joint appearance at her house was a coincidence.

Gray's hand clenched the rope attached to Cali's makeshift collar, giving a clue that he'd like to mete out his own version of justice for the fright that man had given her. She hoped he didn't get an opportunity to come face-to-face with the prowler and that the police would catch him before Gray did. It pleased her to know that he still felt those protective urges toward her.

She glanced at her watch. There was still plenty of time before their appointment. "Even if identifying Cali doesn't lead us to the prowler, I hope we find her owner. She's a great dog. They'll be thrilled to get her back."

Gray's focus was on safety, but hers was on the prospect of a happy reunion between animal and human. But her number-one desire was for a reunion between two humans.

She looked up and caught him studying her. Could he see in her eyes how much she wanted them back together? Quite honestly, she'd rather be standing here with him, holding a plastic bag for a dog, than doing any of the other activities she'd tried to lose herself in since he returned home.

She reluctantly turned her attention from Gray to Cali. "You're a good girl!" She stooped to give Cali a hug and wished the recipient was Gray and that he, rather than the dog, was covering her face with kisses. "We're going to go inside now and get your shoulder all fixed up," she said. "We're going to take good care of you."

Gray watched, apparently taking in her enthusiasm for doing what was best for Cali. "How many underdogs have you rescued since I've been gone?" Without waiting for an answer, he quickly amended his question. "How many four-footed ones and how many two—?"

She rose to her feet and didn't answer, but she knew what he was talking about. She had been the one who'd banded the girls together to share the risks, joys and profits of opening a new business, thereby rescuing all of them from the stuffy corporate jobs that might have awaited them upon graduation…jobs that all of them would have hated.

"That's something I've always liked about you," Gray said, as if he needed to make it clear he was not criticizing but complimenting her.

Liked. They had started toward the front door of the veterinary office, but Ruthie stopped in her tracks. She couldn't let this elephant that was standing between them continue to grow. At some point, they needed to get their issues out in the open. With plenty of time before their appointment, there was no time like the present.

Softly, tentatively, she said, "Liked. You can't even say the word *love*." Rather than give him an opportunity to argue the point, she emphasized, "We *did* love each other."

Gray steeled his jaw. Moved toward the door, but Ruthie stopped him with a hand to his sleeve.

"Go ahead and admit it," she urged. "What does it hurt to admit that we once had something very good? Very special. Perhaps it would take away some of this awkwardness that exists between us if we just got it out there."

He clearly didn't want to go there, but she could be just as stubborn.

"Are you saying you didn't love me?" She paused,

and when a sigh was the best answer she could get from him, she pushed on. "You *did* love me. You told me so many times, even in that awful letter you sent."

"Look, I'm sorry—"

"I'm not asking for an apology. You did what you felt was right at the time." She toed a crack in the sidewalk, and Cali read the gesture as an invitation to sit on her foot. "I'd be lying if I said it didn't hurt."

"You have every right to be angry."

"You don't understand. I was never angry about the breakup. Confused, hurt and bewildered, yes. But never angry."

In the stages of loss and grief, she'd gone through denial, bargaining and depression, but never anger. And certainly not the final stage…acceptance. Always, always, she had believed they'd get back together someday. But that would not happen until they swept the emotional clutter—the *ranzatsu*—out of the way.

"The day your letter came, I was at church, waiting for Bible study to begin. Sobo handed me your letter. She and Pop tried to pretend they weren't watching me while I read it, but I could feel them waiting for whatever good news you might have sent."

Gray groaned and shifted where he stood, but he made no move to leave. To try to escape.

"It was devastating," she said, pulling no punches. "For me. For your grandparents, parents and sister." She wasn't telling him this to hurt him in repayment for the pain he'd caused all of them. She was telling him because it had weighed so heavily on her heart these past four years. The only way she could begin to let go of the hurt was to confront its source.

Gray initially stood mute, and it was clear he didn't know how to respond.

Maybe it wasn't a very nice thing to think, but part of her was glad he was finally experiencing a fraction of the discomfort she'd felt on that fateful day.

Gray seemed to finally find his tongue. "My family always cared a lot for you."

She ignored his sidestepping and turned the subject back to the Dear Jane letter. "Maybe the breakup doesn't compare to what you faced in Afghanistan, but hurt is hurt. I loved you, and you destroyed me."

He looked down at his feet, then met her eyes. "I know, and I'm sorry. I told you in the letter how I felt."

"That was a beginning," she acknowledged, "but we've never fully cleared the air. We've only danced around the subject. It would help to actually address it head-on."

The leash twisted in Gray's large hand. When she turned her attention to the nervous gesture, he stilled his fingers and asked gently, "Are you sure you want to hash this out?"

More sure than she'd ever been. It might hurt to dig down to the truth and expose it to the light of day, but knowing where they'd skidded off course wouldn't hurt as much as wondering and waiting. She nodded.

"Okay," he said, as if considering the repercussions of going into their past. "You're always taking in strays. Always protecting others." He motioned toward Cali, who lifted her ears to a woman exiting the small veterinary office with a cat in a carrier. "Protecting this dog from the pound." Then he motioned toward the vet's front door to emphasize his next point. "Protecting her from rabies."

"Right," Ruthie agreed. "And for four years, I've been protecting you by not forcing a showdown."

A muscle twitched in his jaw while he considered what she'd said. Quietly, he said, "Yes, and how is what you're doing any different from my wanting to protect you?"

Protect her from what? She needed to know, even if only to put the past behind them so they could move on. However, she didn't want to move on. The problem was that when he set his mind to something, there was nothing anyone could do to change his stubborn mind…or heart.

"You haven't changed," she said.

He gave a tug on Cali's leash to distract her from the cigarette butt someone had carelessly tossed to the ground. "And neither have you," he said, then murmured something under his breath that sounded like "please don't."

Don't what? Don't change? Hope skittered through her chest and landed directly on her heart. A smile pulled at the corners of her mouth. Other than addressing the problem he struggled with and refused to share, she didn't want him to change, either.

"Tomorrow please come join us for the Sunset Blessings gathering." Prompted by his hesitation, she added, "The others have been asking about you."

"Don't you think if I do, they'll assume we're involved again?"

That was the whole point. If she and Gray spent enough time together, perhaps they would indeed become involved again.

"Since when," she asked to redirect his focus, "did you start worrying about what other people think?"

Chapter Seven

By that afternoon, Ruthie was the proud new owner of a basic alarm system on her house, and now Gray was working on putting one in at the shop. Distracted by his presence and by Savannah, who was keenly aware of her fixation with their self-appointed security man, she tried to turn her attention to the items that had cluttered her counter for the past week. The situation with Sobo, the doll and, of course, Gray had interfered with her usual fastidious organization, and she was determined to rectify that before the day was done. She had put a lot of time into searching for the woman who'd bought the doll, and now she took a moment to tidy the temporarily neglected shop.

She positioned herself behind the counter, where she could watch the door for customers while she worked. Cali automatically moved with her, circling out a comfy spot on the old blanket Ruthie had brought in for that very purpose. She told herself the added advantage of being able to subtly peek at Gray while he installed the security device had nothing to do with her decision, but the truth was that he offered the best view in the shop.

He had dressed for manual labor today, wearing faded jeans and a pale blue button-front shirt with his company's name embroidered over the pocket. The sleeves had been pushed up to expose lean, corded forearms perfectly suited for wielding power tools, rescuing injured dogs and holding a woman in a way that made her feel like the most beautiful person on earth. He might have been dressed like an ordinary workman, but he was anything but ordinary.

God's time. Sobo had often reminded her prayers weren't answered as quickly as she'd like. Be patient, the elderly woman had urged, just as Paul advised in the book of Galatians. Some translations referred to the fourth aspect of the fruit of the spirit as forbearance, which Ruthie thought of as holding up under a heavy burden. Yep, that fit. And another version called it long-suffering. To her way of thinking, four years of heart suffering had been long enough.

God's time. Right.

She had read the promise in that verse from Jeremiah—"plans to give you hope and a future"—and knew she needed to remain steadfast in that promise. But it wasn't easy to push aside her impatience and, yes, a little anger at how long it was taking Gray to get his act together and realize that he'd thrown away the best thing that had ever happened to either of them.

It also annoyed her that being together in proximity to each other—yet not together as a couple—didn't seem to bother him at all while it was tearing her up inside. So close and yet a thousand miles apart.

She sighed heavily and tamped down her frustration. Perhaps it might help "God's time" pass a little faster if she turned her attention to getting this inventory logged into the computer and placed on display for sale.

She poked through the remaining two boxes of Pop's, stickered each item with a consignment code and set them in piles according to the area of the shop where they would be displayed. Then she pushed the empty box to the floor and a small, colorful object fell along with it.

Ruthie bent to retrieve the thin wallet and was instantly enthralled by the rich colors and vibrant images stitched on the silk cover. Against a background of royal blue to represent a gently rippling pond, several lovely dragonflies of varying sizes and shapes hovered over a shiny koi fish that watched from beneath the silk-stitched waters, while other dragonflies perched delicately on a brilliant pink lotus blossom. The craftsmanship was superb, and she had no doubt this little treasure would sell quickly even at a hefty price. But after the incident with Sobo's doll, Ruthie deemed it wise to check first and make sure this piece was actually intended for sale.

She opened the wallet to discover it was not a wallet after all but a checkbook cover or, in this case, an elegant jacket for a purse-size calendar. A flip of the current-year calendar revealed a few handwritten entries, all carefully penned in Japanese script.

The whine of a hand drill sounded from the door where Gray installed the sensor. She waited until he finished drilling to call him over. On the other side of the shop, Savannah raised her head from a pile of white lace and organza on the sewing machine and flashed a knowing grin.

Gray ambled over to Ruthie's counter, his movements precise and fluid, making her wish she was as easy and relaxed about being in his company as he appeared to be in hers. The *thump-thump-thump* of Cali's tail against her leg matched the ridiculous pounding of her heart.

"This was with the boxes Pop brought in," she said. "Do you think Sobo meant to sell it, or should I hold it back?"

He reached for the calendar and perused the pages. "It wouldn't make sense to get rid of a calendar only a few months into the year."

Savannah wandered over, supposedly to see what they were looking at, but Ruthie suspected she just wanted to see what was going on between the two of them. A matchmaker at heart, Savannah had once urged her friends to sign up for an online-dating service. The timing of the suggestion had been wrong for Ruthie, having come just a few months after Gray's now-infamous letter, so she had declined. Paisley also refused, insisting that she preferred to meet people the old-fashioned way…in person. Savannah's date had been an image-obsessed guy who wanted not only a gorgeous blond beauty, for which Savannah totally fit the bill, but a fitness partner who was willing to enter and run local races with him. Not likely to happen, considering her bum foot. And Nikki's best match had been a clock-and-watch collector who didn't mesh in the romance department but who turned into a friend and eventually became one of her best repair customers.

Soon afterward, Savannah turned her matchmaking

efforts toward volunteering at a child adoption agency. But that didn't stop her from occasionally trying to maneuver people she cared about into each other's arms. And she definitely cared about both her and Gray.

"More hats?" Savannah innocently inquired. She reached down and rubbed Cali's velvety ears.

"No, it's just Sobo's calendar cover. We were trying to decide whether she really wanted to sell it or if Pop had put it in the box by mistake. My guess is it's too pretty to sell. I would want to keep it."

Savannah followed her gaze to the silk-stitched cover in Gray's hands. "What a coincidence. That design looks exactly like the purse that belongs to the elegant Asian woman who came in here last week. You know, the one who bought Mrs. Bristow's doll."

Gray's head jerked up, and his gaze met Ruthie's. He obviously had the same thought she did.

She grabbed Savannah by the arm. "Are you *sure* those dragonflies are exactly like the ones on that woman's purse? It doesn't just sort of look like it, does it?"

Savannah looked down at Ruthie's hand on her arm, and Ruthie let go. "Not *sort* of like it. *Exactly* like it. She set her purse on the counter right here," she said, and motioned to the area where the boxes had sat just minutes ago. "And she proceeded to rummage through the boxes, which I thought was funny because of the way she was dressed."

Ruthie tilted her head in a wordless question.

"She was dressed in a super-nice designer suit, carrying a museum-quality hand-stitched purse. Even her voice and the way she carried herself were elegant," Savannah said, "but there she was, digging through a box of dusty hand-me-downs, looking for all the world like she'd found a priceless treasure."

For one thing, the items in the box had not been dusty. Ruthie could attest to that. Sobo would have been horrified if Pop had passed along anything to sell that was in less-than-perfect condition. As for a finely dressed customer searching through previously owned items—yes, treasures—in her shop, that kind of thing happened all the time. The Carytown shopping area drew customers from a wide variety of social backgrounds and economic means.

"When she found the doll," Savannah continued, "she got so excited and her hands shook so bad I thought she was having a seizure. Once we settled on a price, she couldn't get the money out of her purse fast enough. She dropped her lipstick, her cell phone, then her keys. It was almost comical to watch."

By now Ruthie's hands were starting to shake, and she noticed that Gray's brows had drawn together. Perhaps he'd made the same connection she had.

"Do you suppose she might have dropped the case while she was getting out her money?"

"Honey, I wouldn't have been surprised if she had dropped her teeth, she was that excited."

Ruthie turned to Gray. "How rusty is your Japanese? Can you see if her name is in the book?" With a name to go on, they'd have a starting place when they searched the phone book.

Gray turned the book over in his hands and scanned the front pages for the writing that was as meticulous as Savannah indicated the customer had been. He shook his head. "There's no identifying information in the front of the book."

"What about the calendar entries? If she had a hair appointment, perhaps the stylist could tell us who she saw that day that matches our customer's description. Better yet, maybe she has an upcoming appointment, and we can meet her where she's scheduled to go."

Savannah stepped back dramatically. "Way to go, Miss Marple."

Gray's finger stopped on yesterday's date. "This is the last entry. Looks like we missed it."

Ruthie's hopes fell. Miss Marple, indeed. They were so close, and yet the possibility of finding the doll seemed so far away. "We can't give up yet," she said, more to encourage herself than to convince him to keep trying. "What does it say?"

"*Obasan*. That means *aunt*." He squinted as he struggled to make out the meaning of the rest of the characters. "One o'clock. And the rest is an address on Belmont Avenue."

"Maybe that's where her aunt lives."

"Or it's where she takes her aunt's poodle to be groomed," he said, a note of defeat edging his voice.

"On a Sunday?"

He scowled at her as if to say, "That again?"

"Whatever the reason she had for writing that address in her book, it's at least worth a try." While she was at it, she wanted to suggest he give God another try.

And her.

He shrugged noncommittally. "I suppose it wouldn't hurt to see what's there."

For one crazy, illogical moment, Ruthie thought he was responding to the thought she dared not voice.

That he wanted to give God another try. Maybe see what still existed between her and him.

Savannah flipped her wrist and checked her watch. "If you two are going to check out that address before the prayer vigil begins, you should leave now." The rational side of her brain kicked in and reminded her that he was still talking about the address, and her heart took yet another plummet.

"Go. I'll take Cali home with me." Savannah wiggled her fingers to shoo them along.

At mention of the prayer vigil, Gray made a small noise in the back of his throat.

Every Monday, their church held a prayer vigil for those in special need, and this week Sobo's name claimed the top of the list. Ruthie and her friends had already planned to attend, and Pop and the rest of the family would certainly be there. All believed in the power of prayer, and they were determined to do whatever they could to help.

They all loved Sobo…Pop the longest and strongest, and of course Gray. But judging by the sound he had made, he wouldn't be at church tonight.

The address on Belmont Street belonged to a modest-looking café that sat next to an orchid shop. The logo on the flag over the neighboring store drew Ruthie's attention and called up a long-ago memory of Gray showing up at the Bristows' house the night of her junior prom with a delicate white flower in a plastic box. He had wrapped the orchid around her wrist and planted a chivalrous kiss on the back of her hand.

She jerked her thoughts back to the present and shaded her eyes against the late-afternoon sun to squint at the little bistro. The striped awning provided a quaint, homey feel, and a sign in the window welcomed diners with promises of seafood and vegetarian fare.

"I don't think her *obasan* lives here," Ruthie said. "Are you sure this is the right place?"

But Gray had already removed the key from the ignition and walked around to open her door. "They offer Sunday brunch until two," he said, pointing to the sign in the window. "The note on the calendar was for one o'clock. Perhaps she and her aunt came here for brunch."

"Good point."

She followed him into the dimly lit interior, where they were met by a college-age fellow who offered to seat them at a booth.

"Actually, we're not here to eat," she said. "We came to ask about a Japanese woman and her aunt who had brunch here yesterday."

"We had a lot of people come in yesterday."

"She may have been driving a vintage Mazda Coupe," Gray said, zeroing in on the facts a man might notice.

That got the guy's attention. A smile stretched across his face. "Yeah. Pale green. It was pretty sweet."

Unfortunately, that was all he could tell them, but confirmation that the woman had been here gave them something to go on. Ruthie flagged down a passing waitress and gave her a description of the woman who'd bought the doll.

"Yeah, the older lady is a regular. The younger one, her niece, offered to take her anywhere she wanted for lunch, but Tomiko insisted on coming here." The waitress straightened her posture. "She always asks to sit at my table."

A breakthrough! Ruthie glanced toward Gray, but his expression revealed only polite interest. This woman had just given them the aunt's first name. Perhaps she knew more information that she could share.

Ruthie asked if she knew the niece's name or where either of them lived.

"No, but the niece's house is going to be on the Museum District Mother's Day tour this year. They're both really excited about that."

Gray tipped the woman for the information and handed her his business card. "Would you call me the next time she comes in? It's important that we speak to her."

The waitress turned the bill over in her hand and gave him an appreciative nod.

Back in the car, Gray started the engine and cruised slowly through the neighborhood where the car-club president said he'd seen the woman's vehicle. Unfortunately, the fading daylight quickly made it too dark for a search. Besides, it was probably sheltered in a garage.

Despite the disappointment of learning neither the name of the doll's purchaser nor the location of her car and thus her house, Ruthie could hardly contain her enthusiasm. "If I had decent phone reception, I'd look up the house tour on Google right now. Maybe the niece's address is on the website."

"Maybe later," Gray said. "I've got to drop you off at home, then take Pop to church."

She might be pushing too hard, but she had to ask, "Will you be staying for the vigil? It would be nice if you could be there for Sobo."

He kept his gaze on the road, and for a moment only the twitch of the muscle in his jaw indicated he had heard her.

It may have been a stupid question, she conceded. If he no longer believed in God, why would he think being there could do anything to help his grandmother? She tried another tactic.

"For Pop, then. It would mean a lot to him if you went inside and sat with him." She didn't even ask him to pray. Just sit.

This time, he met her gaze, his brown eyes as serious as she'd ever seen them. "I'll be back to pick him up after the praying is over."

Ruthie's heart sank. He might not stick around for the vigil tonight, but what he didn't know was that the praying would never be over. Not Pop's. Certainly not hers.

If prayers were weapons, she'd aim hers at him until the high-vaulted barriers he'd erected around himself four years ago finally came down.

Gray wished he could have powered past the resistance that held him back from the prayer meeting. Ruthie was right that Pop needed his loved ones around him while they pooled their love and prayers toward Sobo's healing. But he just couldn't bring himself to do it. If duty toward family hadn't been so firmly instilled in him, Gray would have just pulled up to the front of the church, let Pop out and driven off. But he couldn't do that. Instead, he pulled into the parking lot and walked with him to the front of the church.

His grandfather's normally rugged complexion

seemed to have faded over the past week. Although Pop had floated a test balloon and asked if he would stay for the service tonight, there had been no pressure in his question. But his expression told him how strongly he wanted him there. As much as he loved and respected his grandfather, he just couldn't do it. Couldn't be a hypocrite. Couldn't lie and pretend to believe in the prayers that Pop found comfort in.

They were climbing the steps to the portico when one of the heavy front doors eased open and Ruthie leaned out, her red hair draping like a fine silk curtain. "Good, you're here," she said to Pop, but her eyes remained fixed on Gray. "We saved you a seat up front."

Pop kissed her and mumbled something that sounded like "talk some sense into the boy." He went inside and shut the door behind him.

Ruthie pulled the heavy green sweater she wore around herself and leaned against the white porch column. "I'm sorry if I came across a little pushy this afternoon. I was hoping you would come for Pop, even if not for yourself. But you have your reasons, and I respect that." She glanced down at her fingernail and plucked at it with her thumb. "Whatever the cause, something happened that frightened you away from the church."

Her voice grew softer, and he could almost hear the words that remained unspoken: *and me.* It tore him up every time he thought of how much he had hurt her.

"I'm not afraid of the church."

Ruthie was filling in the blanks as well as she knew how. He owed her an explanation. He needed to justify— to her as well as to himself—what he had done.

She stepped forward, reached for his hand, then seemed to think better of it and let her arm drop to her side. "Then explain it to me. Tell me what's bothering you."

Her tone was as kind as when she had soothed Cali after the injury. Soft. Caring. Infinitely patient.

She tugged the knitted sleeves down to cover her hands and pressed her elbows to her sides.

"Go inside," he said just as gently. "You're cold."

She looked as chilled as he sometimes felt inside. He had heard that when people get frostbite, the thawing of the blackened, shriveled skin hurt more than the actual freezing. All the more reason to stay frozen where he was. If it hurt this bad now, what might his blackened, shriveled heart feel like if he let the warmth back in? Either her warmth or God's.

"I'd rather stay out here with you." She gazed at him, her eyes questioning whether he'd stay here with her or send her back to the others…and to the God he no longer believed in.

He pulled off his jacket and wrapped it around her shoulders. The temptation to leave his arms around her hit him hard. It was only with great willpower that he managed to step away.

"To talk me into going inside with you?" He hadn't meant to sound so cynical. It was as if that brief moment of physical closeness had pried open a long-shut door to something inside that he felt shouldn't be examined. Because if he did examine it, he'd start questioning whether he'd done the right thing after all.

Ruthie blinked at the harshness of his tone but pretended she hadn't noticed. He hoped she didn't think it was aimed at her. Even though she reminded him of everything he used to believe and had since given up, he held no grudge against her.

"To hear what caused you to lose your faith." She paused, and her thoughts seemed to drift to the past. "Besides your overwhelming need to protect others, loyalty is one of your greatest virtues. Once you've committed to someone or something, you don't turn your back on them. Whatever it was, it must have been big to cause you to shut God out."

And to shut her out. She was right. It had been hard. Almost as hard as it would have been to try to play the role of someone who still believed…in both God and the possibility of a relationship with her. Neither was a satisfactory solution as far as he was concerned, but shutting them out was more honest than faking a faith he no longer possessed.

From within the church, an organ started to play the opening music. Though no one sang the words, he heard them in his head. *Softly and tenderly Jesus is calling, calling for you and for me.*

He had known the day would come when he would have to pull out those terrible memories and go over them with her. But not today. It wasn't something he could tell her in a sentence or two. If she asked questions, which he was certain would happen, he didn't know if he'd have the answers. "It's a long story. Too long to go into here."

Come home! Come home! Ye who are weary, come home!

"You should go inside," he said. "We'll talk later."

Ruthie tilted her head, her expression serious. "You'll tell me everything? Even if it hurts me?" She slowly let out her breath. "I'd rather know the truth than keep wondering."

Wordlessly, he nodded his promise to tell her all that she wanted to know. Even if it hurt her…even if it hurt him. He owed her that much. He hadn't been ready to explain it in the letter, or even after he had returned home. It wasn't fair to continue to keep her in the dark.

He had locked away the memory of that fateful day, unwilling to examine the ugliness of what had happened…unwilling to ponder the what-ifs, because examining the event under a microscope wouldn't bring anyone back. Wouldn't make a tragic situation right. But if opening the door to that memory could somehow make her feel better about the decision he had thrust upon her, then it would be worth the pain of walking through it again so she could see what had made his heart turn cold.

"We'll talk," he promised. "But now you should go inside."

Slowly, almost reluctantly, she shrugged off his jacket, turning her cheek toward the collar as it slid off her shoulders. She returned it to him, still warm from her body, and slowly pulled open the door. Then she stepped inside and paused in the threshold, her gaze trapping his as she held the door open behind her…a clear invitation to follow.

Come home. Come home…

She turned to face him again. "Even though you rejected God," she said quietly, "He will never turn His back on you."

With that, they parted ways. Ruthie let the door ease closed behind her, all the while looking over her shoulder as if hoping he would change his mind and follow her.

He watched until the final click of the latch echoed into the night. Then he started back down the stairs he had walked up with Pop.

At the bottom, he turned and looked back at the familiar building, driven by an overwhelming urge he could not explain. An urge to reach for something he couldn't express, to ask for understanding with an unanswerable question, to replace the pain and turmoil he had experienced ever since Afghanistan with the peace and acceptance that were so openly visible in Sobo, Pop and especially Ruthie. He imagined her holding hands with Pop, the two of them gathering strength from each other and God, and wished he could draw on that strength. Wished he hadn't been disappointed in God and that he still carried the confidence that showed in Ruthie and the others in the church…confidence that their prayers would be answered.

The song had finished, but the refrain echoed in his heart. *Come home.*

Automatically, as if pulled by tattered threads of the past that still clung to his heart, he placed one foot on the bottom step and slowly lifted his weight up to scale the first of the four steps. Four years. Four blocks of concrete and brick that separated him from God and Ruthie.

One step away from the top, he paused and considered what would be fixed by his going inside to pray with his loved ones. Would it make Sobo better? A strangled sound escaped his throat. It hadn't helped Jakey Rayner when they had needed God most. Gray might be cold inside, but Rayner was even colder, four years in the ground. His had certainly been a misplaced faith.

Gray looked away from the church, unable to turn to a God he didn't believe existed. And in the end, he walked away.

Chapter Eight

A couple of days later, Ruthie stood in the Connecting Threads shop, trying to get Savannah to accept payment for fixing the loose band on Sobo's hat. Unfortunately, her friend refused to accept the cash Ruthie thrust upon her and kept diverting the subject back to Gray's conspicuous absence from the prayer vigil.

"Pastor John saw him leave church the other night. He was hoping Gray would stay for prayer time. I think he wanted to know why he didn't hang around."

There had been four years of nonattendance on Gray's part, so Pastor John clearly knew, even without Sobo and Pop saying so, that something had been keeping him from church. Like her, he had hoped Gray had experienced a change of heart. The pastor's hope had been her own. "What did you tell him?"

"The truth. That I didn't know."

She pressed her lips together, then forced herself not to judge his decision. Gray had promised he would tell her what had made him turn away. Now she just had to trust that he would keep his promise and that God would give her the heart to hear Gray's explanation and the right words to respond. "Well, despite his absence, the prayers are making a difference," she assured her friend. "Sobo has made significant progress and should be able to go home soon."

When they had heard the good news at the hospital last night, Gray had worried about the stress it might cause his grandmother if she returned home and noticed the doll was missing. They both agreed they needed to step up their efforts to find it.

Savannah dragged the dress form from the entry of her shop to the small raised platform where brides, prom goers and other customers modeled their purchases and the alterations she provided for them. "Time for a new fitting," she said. "I changed out the zipper for pearl buttons, and I want to see if they line up properly."

Ruthie stuffed the cash back into her pocket and decided she would find another way to pay Savannah for the hat repairs. "Sorry, not today." When the wannabe bridal designer started to persist, she added, "I'm just not in the mood. Why don't you have Paisley or Nikki model it for you?"

"Come on. You're the closest to my size. Besides, Paisley's getting ready for the lunch crowd, and there's only one customer in your area."

Closest to her size only if she padded the top and hips. "Exactly," she said, focusing on the lone customer. "And I need to wait on her."

"She's browsing," Savannah countered. "Let her shop in peace. If she wants to buy something while you're all trussed up, I'll wait on her."

After a bit more back-and-forth, she agreed, but only on the condition Savannah would take payment for the hat without complaining. The perky blonde plucked the bills from her hand and stuffed them into her sewing machine drawer. Now Ruthie was her hostage for the fifteen or twenty minutes it would take Savannah to ooh and aah over her own creation.

She slipped into the changing booth and came out feeling like a princess in a Disney movie. She ran a hand down the front of the dress and reveled in the luxurious feel of the fabric. "How long have you been working on this?"

"Since I was fourteen and learned to sew my first seam in home ec class."

Ruthie turned her back to Savannah and listened to the history of the dress while her friend buttoned the hundred or more tiny pearls from neck to hip. Savannah had started with a basic A-line dress, and as her skills grew, so had the details, embellishments and alterations on the garment. And as Savannah had grown curves, she had let out seams and added strategic and artistically designed inserts to accommodate her lush figure. Some brides might consider the dress to be a tiny bit overdone, but the layers of fabric and thoughtful attention to neckline, sleeves and even parts that weren't seen reflected the depth, creativity and multi-layered personality of the future bride.

"When will you know the dress is finished?" Ruthie asked.

Savannah laughed. "When I meet the man who's smart enough to ask me to marry him." She eyed her carefully, taking in her slim figure with an experienced designer's eye. "Let me make a wedding dress for you. I'll start puttering with it in my spare time, and by the time you need it, it will be ready."

The last time Savannah had made that offer, Ruthie had been engaged to Gray. They'd gotten only as far as preliminary sketches of the dress when Ruthie received the breakup letter. The design her friend had come up with, however, had been the stuff of fairy tales. Unfortunately, her relationship with Gray had not ended with a fairy-tale wedding. "That's not necessary, but thank you for the sweet thought."

"If it was necessary, it wouldn't be a gift. I'll just take your measurements after you slip out of the gown. Then you can tell me what kind of fabrics and styles you like."

Ruthie shook her head at her friend's persistence. "I'll have middle-age spread by the time I'm ready to use it, so you may as well wait."

Though she joked it off, she yearned for her own wedding and her own fairy-princess bridal gown. Most of all, she yearned for a bridegroom who would look at her with such love and affection that she would turn into a sentimental puddle right there before the altar. A groom with nearly black hair and kind brown eyes who saw all her secrets and loved her anyway.

The bell over the door jangled to announce the arrival of another customer.

She needed to get out of this dress and back to work, but first she wanted to finish the little fantasy that played out in her head. She turned back to the mirror and imagined herself with a bouquet of anemones of various colors. Daisy, who loved all things floral and had even chosen her own nickname, had told her the anemone stood for faith and belief.

Beside her would be a tall, handsome groom who was strong in everything he did. A man who unflinchingly adhered to his values, revered God and committed for a lifetime to her and the children they would raise together.

As if her thoughts had morphed into flesh, Gray appeared beside her in the mirror. Instead of a tux, he wore a dark suit that emphasized the breadth of his shoulders and the narrowness of his waist. And even though she stood on the raised platform, he stood a couple of inches taller. Gray stared back at her in the mirror as if he had just read all of the silly thoughts that had played out in her imagination. His expression flickered between curiosity, amusement and nervous uncertainty.

Awkward. The word didn't begin to describe how she felt right now. It was worse than being caught as a teenager dancing on the bed and singing into a hairbrush.

Self-conscious about having traveled to that fondly wished-for wedding scenario, she turned and stepped off the platform.

Gray came forward and lifted a supportive arm as she descended. After she was safely back on the worn hardwood floor, he stepped back and slanted an inquisitive gaze at her. His eyes raked over the incriminating layers of white. Did he think she'd recently gotten engaged? And if so, how did he feel about that?

A foolish part of her hoped he was upset. Maybe even kicking himself for letting her go. He opened his mouth as if to say something, then clamped it closed and silently waited her out.

"I, um…"

Ever the matchmaker, Savannah piped up. "Doesn't she make a beautiful bride?"

Gray granted her a thin smile, his only response, then turned back to Ruthie.

"This is Savannah's dress. She asked me to model it for her so she could check the fit."

Ruthie caught his gaze flicker almost imperceptibly between her and her friend, and a hint of incredulity dusted his features. Okay, so Savannah wasn't officially engaged yet, either. Not even dating, in fact. She could understand how it might raise an eyebrow that her friend was already working on a dress.

"I found the house," he said, changing the subject and removing the need for further explanation about the dress. "It's the only one described on the website as having an Asian influence in the decor. I drove past there on the way over, and there's a garage behind the house. Probably with an old Mazda Coupe parked inside."

"You didn't stop?"

He was as anxious as she to get Sobo's doll back, yet he'd driven right past the house where he knew it might be? That didn't make sense.

"I thought the lady might be more receptive to opening the door if you went along, especially since the prowler hasn't been caught yet. A man by himself might raise suspicion."

Savannah emitted a tiny hiccup of a laugh. "In that suit, she's more likely to mistake you for an insurance salesman."

Ruthie eased past him toward the shop entrance. "Sure. Let me get my purse."

Gray stopped her with a hand to her upper arm. His strong fingers were gentle, but they crushed the white lace sleeves. "Perhaps you should change rather than go looking like somebody's bride."

On their way to the house on Monument Avenue, Gray couldn't stop thinking about Ruthie in that dress. Sure, it sagged a little in some areas, but the image she'd branded onto his mind had been that of a willowy red-haired waif who could bring a man to his knees merely by peeking at him through those ridiculously long eyelashes.

It had been almost like a glimpse into the past—of what might have been. Had circumstances been different, he might have waited near the altar of the church he'd fled two nights ago, Rayner standing beside him all decked out in his best man getup, and watched the most beautiful woman in the world walk down the aisle toward him. And he would have been saying "I do" and kissing the bride instead of "I don't" and wishing for kisses that would never come.

Distracted, he forgot to watch for the house number until Ruthie shot forward in the passenger seat and pointed to a stately house on the corner. "Is that it?"

He slowed in time to see that the number matched, then pulled into a parking spot in front of the neighboring house. "How did you know?"

She lifted a shoulder. "The sculpted shrubs, meditation pool and rock garden gave it away."

They got out of the car, and Gray took a moment to study the brick home. It did have an Asian flair to its simple landscape. As they approached the house, more telltale signs hinted that they'd reached the right one: a bird bath with a ceramic water lily in the center, a wind chime with Japanese characters in place of the more typical metal tubing and a flower box with an upward-pointing roof to shade the new spring blossoms.

He pressed the doorbell, and the melodic sound carried outside. A fluffy white dog bounced near the narrow curtained window beside the door and yapped to announce their arrival.

"Did you bring a picture of Sobo?" Ruthie asked.

He shook his head, then pushed his hair back in place. "Why would I do that?"

"Seeing a person's face helps strangers identify with them. If the customer sees the doll as being returned to a likable person, she might be more willing to sell it back to us. Besides, who could look at Sobo's sweet smile and not like her?"

The inner door opened, and a pretty fiftysomething woman peered at them through the storm door. She was every bit as elegant as the others had described her, with chin-length brown hair falling in soft waves around her face and smooth skin that made her appear younger than her years. Her voice was so soft she could barely be heard over the dog's barking.

"Yes?"

Gray hoped the website had listed the name of the house's owner correctly. If he got it wrong, he might come across as rather shady. "Are you Amaya Kagawa?" At her subtle nod, he felt encouraged. "I'm Gray Bristow, and this is—" Here he went again. That awkward introduction. "—my friend Ruthie Chandler. We're here to ask if you—"

"I don't want to buy. Thank you very much." The woman dipped her head in a slight bow and started to push the door closed.

Ruthie eased past him. "Wait, Mrs. Kagawa! I own

Gleanings, the shop in Carytown where you bought the Japanese doll. The doll in the red silk dress."

The door opened again. This time, the customer gently nudged the dog back with her foot and stepped outside. She glanced toward the sidewalk as if to check whether anyone else was in the area, leading Gray to wonder if she suspected they might have henchmen lurking nearby. Perhaps he'd better let Ruthie do the talking.

"The doll belongs to his grandmother." Ruthie went on to explain how Pop had mistakenly brought a box of Sobo's and his personal belongings to the store to be sold. She even described Sobo's troubles with her broken hip and subsequent hospitalization, not details he would have thought to share but which seemed to garner some sympathy from Mrs. Kagawa. "It's the only thing she has left from her childhood. So we were wondering if you would sell the doll back to us. We'll give you double what you paid for it."

He suspected Mrs. Kagawa might be swayed by sympathy for Sobo's plight, but judging from this house and its location on Richmond's historic Monument Avenue, money was probably not the best motivator for her.

"I'm so sorry. It is a gift for my *oba*. My aunt. Her birthday party is in two Saturdays, and I know the doll is the only thing she would want."

Gray fisted his hands. They were this close. He and Ruthie had searched relentlessly to find the doll, and now they couldn't just walk away without it. "What if we buy you another one?" he suggested. "An even nicer doll that's brand-new. I can have it shipped to you overnight so you'll receive it in plenty of time for the party."

She reached for the doorknob, and from inside, the dog resumed its yapping. "I wish I could help you."

He decided now was the time to pull out the big guns, and he named a figure that even the uppermost crust of the ritziest Monument Avenue residents would consider long and hard. But Mrs. Kagawa apologetically shook her head.

Ruthie looked at him as if to ask whether he had any other ideas up his sleeve.

Unfortunately, he could think of nothing other than giving her his card. Considering how she had warmed up to Ruthie, he jotted her name, the name of the shop and her phone number in case Mrs. Kagawa felt more comfortable calling her if she changed her mind.

He handed her the card and asked her to call either of them if she thought of anything else her aunt would rather have for her birthday.

"Thank you," the woman said, and accepted the card with a slight bow. Something told him it might go into the trash before he and Ruthie even made it back to the car. "I hope your *obaasan* is better soon."

The door closed with a final click, and the dog's frenzied yapping quieted almost immediately. As they turned to descend the porch steps, he offered his elbow to Ruthie. She curled her fingers around the crook of his arm and he gave them a gentle squeeze. Together they would think of something.

They had to.

Even after they reached the sidewalk, Ruthie clung to his arm. Grateful for his chivalry, she let him walk her to the passenger side of the car and open the door for her. The frustration of having come so close to regaining the precious doll only to have their very generous offers politely refused chipped away at the composure she'd been fighting to hold on to ever since Gray had shown up in her life again a little over a week ago. Tears burned at the corners of her eyes, and she blinked them back as she settled onto the leather seat.

Gray got in and put the key in the ignition, then looked at her and dropped his hand without turning it. "Are you all right?"

He was so sweet. So caring and understanding. And that was her undoing. His low-voiced concern brought to mind the night he had shown her his orders to deploy to Afghanistan. He had been more worried about her reaction than about the risky situation he was about to enter.

"I'll be okay," she said, her voice choking on the words. "It's Sobo who's sick and vulnerable and missing a piece of her past. There's nothing I can do. Nothing else either of us can do. It just makes me so…" She lifted a hand to brush away the tears that threatened to roll down her cheek. Her fingers shook. "So angry. But what makes me even angrier is that there's no one to be angry with. Mrs. Kagawa bought the doll fair and square, and she has every right to refuse our offers to buy it back."

She drew in a breath and let it out on a shaky sigh.

"I don't blame her," she continued. "It's a beautiful doll, in excellent condition. I'd want to keep it, too."

Gray reached over and grasped her hand, bridging the distance between them. "There's still time before the party next weekend. Maybe I'll come back tomorrow and give her a picture of Sobo, like you suggested."

She wanted to hold on to hope that her customer's mind could be so easily changed after having turned down all their other offers. But reality whispered that they'd done all they could. That the doll was forever lost to them. Lost to Sobo.

"It's no use," she said, a tremble in her voice. "We'll have to tell Sobo that I sold her only remaining child-hood keepsake. She's going to be devastated."

She sniffled, and the last word wobbled crazily off her tongue.

"Hey, come on," Gray murmured. "Stop beating yourself up." He let go of her hand, scooted closer and draped his arm around her shoulder. He gave her a warm squeeze and rested his cheek against the top of her head. "What happened to that mustard grain of faith you always carry around inside you? Aren't you the person who always says you can do anything through God, who strengthens you?"

She didn't know whether it was the warm tone of his voice, the familiar comfort of his arms around her or the fact that despite his own shaken faith he was reminding her of scriptural promises, but whatever it was, it tipped her over from being merely upset to to-tally losing it.

The tears she'd been holding back burst forth and drenched his suit jacket. Ruthie hated that she was ru-ining his clothes—she was embarrassed to have him witness her crying. As a fair-skinned redhead, she al-ways developed ugly red splotches when she cried, and she was sure today was no exception.

Gray retrieved a clean handkerchief and handed it to her. When she was done wiping away the tears, he finished the job by rubbing his thumb gently under her eye.

Great. Not only was she red and splotchy, now she

had mascara all over her face. Strangely, his expression reflected none of her disgust. Instead, his eyes were filled with compassion and...love?

Six months after she had moved in with the Bristows, her mother's birthday had crept up on the calendar and clobbered her all over again with the permanence of her loss. Sobo and Pop had been wonderful to her, treating her the same as their own blood-related grandchildren, so she'd done all she could to hide her sadness from them. She'd thought she had done a pretty good job of hiding it from the extended family as well, but Gray had noticed.

He had cornered her in the kitchen, away from the others, and insisted she tell him what was wrong. He had stroked her face, just as he did now, and told her she wasn't stupid for grieving the mother who'd been so good to her. Nor was she being ungrateful to his grandparents for wishing her mother was still alive. That night, he'd stuck around for dinner, and afterward dessert had mysteriously appeared on the table. A cake flamed with candles, and the scripted icing spelled out her mother's name. Instead of singing the "Happy Birthday" song, they'd all sung, "Love and gratitude to you!" Sobo had added that she and Pop were grateful Ellen had done such a fine job raising their new honorary granddaughter and that they were grateful to offer the finishing touches. And to lighten the mood, Gray had said he was grateful Sobo had a new apple-canning apprentice so he wouldn't have to help out anymore.

His kind words and gentle manner had comforted her then, as they did now. An awareness between them had begun that day—she remembered it on her mother's birthday every year—and now it hung between them, just as thick and warm and sweet as it had been back then.

Gray pulled her closer, and the midday shadow that bristled his jaw lightly scraped against her skin. She felt his soft breath tease a tendril of hair and wished they could stay like this forever. Holding each other, forgetting about what had pushed them apart and just *being* in each other's company.

A moment later, when he lowered his head to kiss away her sadness, she wished they could stay like *this* forever. She returned the kiss, and a flutter of shyness swept over her, just as if this were their first time. It was a chaste kiss, but he took his time, for which she was glad. And when he slowly drew away, she knew that nothing about their feelings for each other had changed. If anything, they'd grown stronger.

The sentiment that flooded her emotions reflected back to her in Gray's eyes. It was too late now to go their separate ways. They were older and wiser and knew their hearts better now. And she could see his acknowledgment as clearly as she felt it in her own heart. From the day she'd first met him, she had felt something persistently drawing them to each other. His eyes, gazing down at her now, could not lie.

Ruthie was elated by the kiss. By the knowledge that he was affected by it…affected by her. By the clarity that, despite that letter he'd written to her, he still wanted her.

On the other hand, Gray still seemed troubled. As if he was torn between kissing her again and bolting from the car.

She squeezed his arm. "You felt it, too. Didn't you?"

He shook his head. Not "No, I didn't feel it," but "No, I don't want to go there."

In his letter he had said he didn't want her to yoke herself to him, an unbeliever. But as Pastor John sometimes said, God can let someone "know with a knowing," and she knew with that kind of certainty that Gray still loved her and that he still believed. Deep down. So deep, perhaps, that he had thought it was gone from him.

His faith had been shaken by something…something she trusted he would share with her soon. But in the Bible, Peter had doubted, too. Jesus had beckoned him to walk on the water, and Peter had noticed the wind and waves. As when Peter focused on the storm around him and began to sink, that was how Gray began to founder.

It was a risk to ask Gray the next question…a risk of scaring him away or of setting herself up to be hurt again. But it was a risk she had to take. Pop had always said, "The best things in life don't come easy." She would always regret it if she let the most wonderful man she'd ever met continue to slip even further away because of something that had happened four years ago. Something that, if he would only open up to her, they might be able to work through. Gray was a good man, and she believed with time, patience and lots of prayer, he would soon return to the God he used to love. And she was willing to stand by him while he traveled the circuitous road back to faith.

"Do you suppose," she ventured, "we could give us another try?"

Chapter Nine

Gray tensed, knowing what she wanted from him. She wanted the full package. A man to love her and adore her and start a family together, all of which he was more than willing to do. But she also wanted him to love God, as she did. To say grace before meals, go to church on Sundays and be faithful to the God who had turned His back on him during his time of greatest need. Those were the deal breakers.

He wasn't ready. Recalling the song he'd heard at church the other night, which still resonated in his head with annoying clarity every time he was alone and quiet, he wanted to answer an unqualified yes. He wanted to *come home* to Ruthie. But he wasn't ready for God. Not yet.

Maybe never.

As much as he wanted God out of his life, he wanted Ruthie in. She watched him, waiting for the answer he wanted to give her but couldn't. Sitting near her like this, their faces so close he could smell the hint of cucumber-and-melon fragrance she loved so much, he fought the crazy urge to count her freckles. Fought to keep from taking her into his arms again and kissing her as if they could somehow, crazily, make up for the years apart.

But even if they could work out the differences in their faith, could they work out the differences that had arisen as a result of his service in Afghanistan?

It had been hard to come home to a "normal" life. Sleep might be replenishing for others, but for him it was a time to relive the unresolved memories of his time overseas. For Ruthie, witnessing a minor fender-bender accident in front of her shop might elicit a prayer and compassionate there-theres. But for him, such sights stirred up nightmares of the elderly man who'd been intentionally run over by a driver too fearful of an ambush to stop and let the man finish crossing the street.

She would never understand what he'd been through. Truth be told, he'd lived through it himself and still didn't understand it. Moments of quiet camaraderie with his fellow soldiers juxtaposed with times of drawn guns and fear. Civilians selling their wares on streets that only hours before had been popping with gunfire. It made no sense. How could *anyone* understand such a way of life?

On the one hand, he found himself growing impatient with the television news reporters whose biggest story lately seemed to be a Peeping Tom who so far had caused no harm. And on the other, he found himself wanting to wrap his loved ones in Bubble Wrap and keep them all safe from even the mere threat of harm.

Was the chasm between them too wide to bridge?

He pulled away and leaned back against the head-rest. Tried not to focus on the hope in her hazel eyes and the possibility that he might break her heart yet again. If they were going to try this again—and he even questioned his sanity in considering it—she needed to understand that she wasn't going to change him. He had been broken during that miserable day in Afghanistan when he'd lost his faith, and he couldn't let her go into this believing she could slap a bandage on him and fix him. He had come home with all his limbs intact, but a big piece of him was missing, never to be regained. He wished he could believe with the naive faith he used to have, but whatever faith had once been there was now so bruised, tarnished and battered it was unsalvageable.

He sighed, the sound so heavy that the restrained eagerness behind her smile wilted just a little.

"There need to be conditions," he said cautiously. Then he rushed forward before she got any wrong ideas. "Primarily that you will not attempt to steer me back to church."

Ruthie jutted her jaw forward while she rolled the idea around in her mind. He knew her well enough and trusted her enough to know that she wouldn't make a promise unless she was certain she could fulfill it.

"What about saying grace before meals?" she asked. "I usually say it out loud, as do Sobo and Pop. And if I break out into spontaneous prayer, I'm going to make an emu hand."

"I'm not asking you to change yourself." He appreciated her sincerity. Appreciated everything about her and wouldn't want to change a thing. "I'm just asking you not to try to change me."

Ruthie grinned. "Is it okay if I ask you to remove your elbows from the table?"

"Hey, somebody's gotta clean me up and make me look nice in public."

"All right, then. It's a deal."

She looked so happy that he wanted to throw caution to the wind and rejoice with her. But he couldn't. Not yet.

"It's not enough that you agree," he said, and her smile abruptly went south. "You need to understand why I sent you that letter. To understand what made me the way I am today."

"Of course. I want to hear all about it," she said. "I want to understand."

A movement over his shoulder caught his attention. Amaya Kagawa had stepped out onto her porch and leaned around the pillar in an effort to see what they were doing in the car so long.

"We're making her nervous." He pulled away from Ruthie and turned the key in the ignition.

And this conversation with Ruthie was making him nervous.

At first Ruthie had thought he was going to take her back to Gleanings and that his explanation would be delayed yet again. Instead, he drove to Maymont Park and pulled under the shade of the tree in the parking lot. Then he led her to the Japanese Garden, where they walked the gravel path in silence.

Her heart soared at the prospect of renovating their tattered relationship. There would be hurdles to overcome, but the major one—Gray's resistance—had been conquered. By comparison, the rest of the hurdles should be easy.

While she and Gray strolled, the pruned trees and

shrubs, raked sand pools, bridges and stone lanterns in the garden brought to mind her visits here with Sobo. She and her honorary grandmother had walked this path together, usually silent but sometimes sharing whatever was on their minds and hearts. At the time, it had seemed as if Sobo was searching for something. Something unspoken and maybe even unrecognized.

Was Gray also searching? Or might that be wishful thinking on her part?

She would agree to his terms, mainly because nagging a person to faith never worked. But she also believed that as they worked through reconnecting, Gray would soon remember the joys they'd experienced in their previous relationship with each other. Perhaps their being together might prompt him to want to reconnect with God, as well.

Patience, she reminded herself. *Don't get ahead of yourself. Don't get ahead of God.* She'd done a lot of praying about her relationship with Gray, and she truly believed God wanted them to be together. Now she just had to practice patience as they worked their way back together.

The sparseness of the Japanese Garden's landscaping reflected her current pared-down relationship with Gray. Simple. Bare. The empty spaces seemed to point to possibilities. The discreet use of flowers and the garden's subtlety in the numerous shades of green, brown and gray reminded her of the need for a light touch when interacting with him. She would still be herself, of course, and her faith would naturally show through, but she'd leave all else to God.

Gray cleared his throat. "There's a lot I can't tell

you," he began at last. "What I *can* say is that we were in the desert, in unfriendly territory."

They continued walking, and he touched her hand as if to hold it, then pulled away. She wanted to reach for him, draw him back to her, but resisted. Gave him the space he seemed to need.

Carefully and cautiously, he opened up and described what had happened on that infamous day.

"Jake Rayner was the only person with me on that assignment," he continued. "We called him Jakey because he was the baby of the group." He paused to give a heartless laugh. "He hated that name. But he was just a kid, and he seemed like a little brother, so I felt responsible for him. After a while we became very close."

She listened while he went on to describe how they'd been driving through a village when they came under fire.

"It was so hot that day it was like looking through rippling waves of air as we drove our jeep near a remote town. I remember looking over at Jakey. The sun glinted down on him and sort of cut him in half with shadow and light. It was kind of a bizarre thing to notice, but for some reason it stood out to me."

He brushed a couple of fallen leaves off a stone bench and waited for her to sit before joining her.

"The air was still, with no dust flying, and the sky was incredibly clear and sharp. You could see for miles." He gazed off as if measuring that remembered vision against what he saw now. "In Virginia, even on the most sunny days, it's not that sharp. Probably because of all the humidity here."

She murmured agreement, letting him talk through

the small things to get to the point of what he wanted to tell her.

"Our jeep got hit by hostile fire. Next thing you know, we were running to take cover behind a mud-brick house that was missing an outer wall from all the shelling that had taken place before. Jakey and I crouched down near a pile of rotten potato peels and scraps of eggplant and tomato. That's when we realized someone still lived in that bombed-out building. As long as I live, I'll never forget that smell of rotting potato." He paused a moment, apparently considering how to continue. "We returned fire. Hit the mark. As far as we could tell, there was only one shooter. That's when I heard a kid from inside the house. In case there were other snipers hiding nearby, we decided to make a run for it…get away from there so we didn't put civilians at risk. And Jakey was going crazy with fear, so I had to get him to safety before he lost his cool and put us in even more danger."

Ruthie realized she was holding her breath, then let it out slowly. Even in the midst of being shot at, his concern had been for the residents of the house and his buddy. She imagined that if she were in that situation, she would be in full panic, unable to think clearly. Yet he had focused on others rather than on his own safety.

"While we were running for our lives," he said, "we could hear the sounds of the outdoor marketplace going on a quarter mile away. For them the gunfire was just another everyday happening." He shook his head. "People shouldn't have to live like that."

Now he grew silent. His fingers opened and closed on his lap as if even today his hands wanted to do something about what had happened back then. Something more. Maybe something different. She didn't know which. All she knew was that it still pained him to think about what had happened.

She slipped her hand into his and squeezed. She wanted to say something to comfort him. Something that let him know how much she sympathized with what he went through. How much she ached for the families—mothers, fathers, children—who lived under such stressful conditions every day. But all the words that came to her sounded lame in her head, so she didn't speak them. Instead, she suggested, "We can finish this another time. There's no need to—"

"No." Gray turned and met her gaze. He pulled her hand up to his lips and gently kissed the backs of her fingers. "This has stood between us long enough. I want to finish."

Then, in opposition to his words, he sat for a long moment saying nothing. He watched the koi fish in the pond, so she watched, too. Their slow, steady movements provided a sense of calm purposefulness. After a few moments, he spoke again.

"When it looked like the area was clear, I grabbed Jakey by the sleeve and we ran for a wall. The whole time, I was operating on adrenaline, thinking only about getting to the next safe place and the one after that. Wondering if we'd be able to make it back to our camp on foot before nightfall, when we'd be the most vulnerable."

Gray let go of her hand to rub the back of his neck.

"While I was relying on the training I'd received and on my own wits, Jakey kept saying over and over, 'Lord, help us. Lord, save us.' Like it was a chant or something. And while we were running for the immediate shelter of the fence, he started in on the Lord's Prayer. We had just thrown ourselves over the fence when he got to 'deliver us from evil.' That's when a grenade went off to the left of us, near Jakey, and he fell to the ground."

Gray looked sick to his stomach. She wanted to stop him from saying more. Spare him from the images that surely haunted him. But he pushed on.

"After I took out the assailant, I dragged Jakey behind that broken wall, where I could take a look at his injuries."

"He was alive?" she asked hopefully.

He clenched his teeth, and his expression hardened. "Just barely. Remember how I said the glint of sun in the jeep had seemed to cut him in half? That's where the shrapnel tore into his chest."

She gasped and drew a hand to her mouth. "No."

He went on to tell of his struggles getting Jakey back to the camp, an hours-long ordeal on foot over several miles of harsh desert. Losing their way, coming upon yet another small village and skirting around it, away from the potential of more enemy fire. Running low on water. And finally encountering a stray dog with its hackles raised, ready to attack.

"I bandaged Jakey up the best I could and somehow managed to get him back to camp." He pressed the heel of his hand against his temple. "Alive."

The tension in her gut eased at the revelation that young Jakey had survived the horrendous ordeal.

"He died less than an hour later."

The news slammed into her, the unfairness of it hitting her like a rock to the temple. "Oh, Gray. I'm so sorry."

She didn't know what else to say. In a situation like this, anything she said would be merely empty words. A hollow echo of a sentiment that was too little, too late. Instead, she touched his arm, wanting to convey her feelings to him without inadequate words.

Gray closed his fingers around hers. "He was barely old enough to shave."

At Jakey's age, Gray had been making eyes at Ruthie, working on homework for his college courses and thinking about a future that he anticipated would span another fifty years or more.

"The kid had never had a chance," he continued. Shortly afterward he'd received another upbeat letter from Ruthie, saying all the things he could no longer believe. And he'd felt guilty that he would eventually be going home to her. "I felt guilty for not—"

No. He refused to go there. Playing "what if" would only mess with his mind and rip further at his gut.

Ruthie watched him, her watery eyes full of compassion. She cared. There was no doubt about that. But she didn't get it. For her to truly understand, she would've had to be there. And he wouldn't wish that on anyone. But maybe he could help her understand why the God thing had hit him so hard.

"Maybe I could have dealt with it better," he ventured, "if the kid hadn't been calling out to God for help. Even after he'd been hit, he was still praying. Mumbling incoherently most of the time, but he was definitely talking to God."

If this had been five years ago—before Jakey died— and he had poured his heart out like this, Ruthie would have offered some comforting Bible verses. He would have accepted them back then, and they would have eased his spirit. But not now. He was grateful she didn't attempt to go there.

She slid her arm around his waist and rested her head against his shoulder. "I'm so sorry, Gray," she said, her voice catching in her throat. "It wasn't fair."

"You're right. It wasn't fair." He put his arm around her shoulders and experienced a moment of guilt at finding comfort in her warmth and caring. "It should have been me."

It was late by the time they returned to Abundance, arriving just in time for Sunset Blessings.

Gray carried a couple of roasted chickens he had picked up from Ellwood Thompson's grocery on their way back. Although Paisley would donate leftover sandwiches and pastries from Milk & Honey, Gray had suggested complementing it with something more substantial for their homeless friends. And when she had commended his thoughtfulness, he had brushed away her praise and mumbled something about buying the chicken to satisfy his own hunger. But she knew better.

Gray hesitated on the sidewalk in front of the shop. "Are you sure you're ready to let people know?" he asked. "They might have some doubts about us, especially after…"

After the way he'd dumped her. "They won't have any doubts," she assured him. "My friends have never said anything against you, and they won't start now."

As for her, she wanted people to know. Now that Gray was back in her life—now that they were back in each other's hearts again—she wanted the whole world to know. Wanted the whole enchilada. Every part of him. Even the part that used to love God but now wavered with doubt.

"Do you have doubts?" she asked in response to his question about announcing that they were back together.

He adjusted the grocery bag in his arm. "Not about you."

Meaning he had doubts about the faith thing. Being honest with herself, she had to admit she was uncertain whether he'd ever come back to God. The possibility saddened her. But there was no doubt he loved her, even if he had trouble saying it at times.

"If you're uncomfortable mentioning we're back together again," she said, "we can just let it slide for now."

Save the announcement until after they'd had a chance to test their newly revived relationship. See if it would last.

He shook his head and set the bag at his feet. Then he pulled her to him and played with a tendril of hair that fell to her shoulder. "They're going to know, whether we tell them or not."

Ruthie glanced over his shoulder at a movement in the store window and thought that if he continued to hold her this close in public—a situation that certainly appealed to her—friends wouldn't need a Sherlock Holmes hat to figure out that something was going on between them.

He seemed to be tiptoeing through land mines, not telling her exactly what he wanted. She supposed he was feeling vulnerable, but she wanted to make sure they were on the same page. And she wanted to know he was certain about what they were reigniting. If he was certain enough to tell her friends, then she would have every confidence there was no doubt in his mind about their picking up where they left off.

"Would you rather people not know?" she persisted. She held her breath. On the one hand, she could understand any reluctance he might have, but on the other, she'd be hurt and maybe a little angry if he wanted to keep their relationship hidden.

Gray dropped his hand from her shoulder and captured her hand. "It's a big step to take, and I want us to be aware that it's a step. Not just trip over it." He paused a moment and looked down at his feet. After a moment, he met her gaze again. "I understand how much I hurt you with that letter. I don't want to hurt you again. If it would be better keeping this quiet rather than have people watch us under a microscope, then I should not attend today's Sunset Blessings with you."

For a second it seemed as though he was backing away again, but the earnestness in his eyes told her his concern was only for her. She squeezed his hand. "I really want you with me, but only if you're ready. I won't push you."

Although she didn't say it aloud, the implication was clear that she wouldn't push religion on him, either.

He smiled and stepped away to open the door. Inside, he looped his arm around her shoulder and walked with her back to the Sunset Blessings gathering.

The next day, Cali met Gray at the door of his grandparents' home. Her tail wagged in greeting, and she opened her mouth in a goofy smile.

He rubbed her neck and slid a hand down her side,

taking in how well the shoulder injury was healing. "Hey there, gal. You been entertaining Pop and Sobo?"

The dog danced happily and led him to Sobo's temporary bedroom, where numerous voices filtered out into the hall. As he approached, he could see there were more than a half dozen people standing around her bed—the next-door neighbor and a couple of ladies from church chatting with Sobo, his parents and uncle talking to each other and Pastor John murmuring something to Ruthie and Pop—and all their voices melded together in a pleasant din. It sounded like a party.

From his vantage point at the door, he saw Sobo propped up in the rented hospital bed. Even from this distance, her complexion was noticeably healthier than it had been a few days ago. Rosier than it had been when he saw her Monday evening after dropping Pop off at church. Now everyone claimed her abrupt turnaround to be a blessing from God as a reward for the earnestness of their prayers. But he knew better. Though he believed Sobo's sudden improvement to be mere coincidence—probably due to happen at that time with or without the addition of prayers—he was sincerely relieved to see her looking so much better.

He and Pop had brought Sobo home from the hospital this morning, and Gray had promised to stop by this evening to check on her progress. Maybe stay the night to help Pop care for her. With plenty of TLC and a bit of luck, she should be back on her feet in a month or so.

Cali led the way into the room, her tail held high as she threaded her way among the visitors to put herself within reach of Sobo's small hand where it hung over the bed rail. At the touch of Cali's fur against her fingertips, his grandmother smiled and rumpled the dog's ears.

Sobo looked up from the brown dog, met his gaze and her smile widened. She lifted her hand from the dog and beckoned him in.

He wondered whether the small room could hold another person but eased his way in anyway and stood beside Ruthie. "Hey," he said to Sobo in particular and to everyone else in general. "What's going on?"

Pop swept a hand toward his wife. "Your grandmother's friends rallied around her during the rough time. She thought it only right that they share her joy over her recovery." Pop slanted a wink at him. "Besides, I think she was ready for some company."

"That's great." Gray found it encouraging that she wanted friends and family around her, but she needed her rest, too. "Let's just make sure she doesn't get overtired."

Sharon, Sobo's friend from the Bible study group, turned and addressed his concern. "Everybody just got here a few minutes ago. We'll keep it short."

Ruthie reached for him, and he took her small hand in his. He had missed this. Missed turning to her no matter what was happening in their lives and always finding her there. Missed her smiles during the good times and the little line of concern between her eyebrows when they shared their troubles. The Sunset Blessings gathering and Sobo's return home today were good ways to restart that.

"Yes, we need to let Naoko get her rest," Pastor John said. "Before we go, let's all join hands and take a moment to offer our thanks for her return home and ask for continued healing."

Around the room hands linked up. He and Ruthie were already holding hands, and now Pastor John reached toward him to complete the circle.

Gray looked down at the outstretched hand. Part of him wanted to join with the others and participate in giving thanks. All he had to do was simply take Pastor John's hand, just as he did with Ruthie. Left or right, it shouldn't make any difference. Unable to move either toward or away from the preacher, he stood in place as if paralyzed.

Involuntarily, he thought of Jakey. What did his buddy have to be thankful for? That God had ignored him despite his desperate pleas for help? And why did these people think God had anything to do with Sobo's healing? Though he was glad she felt well enough to come home, as far as he was concerned, her improvement had been a result of excellent medical care, rest and time. That she perked up so dramatically after their prayers was mere coincidence.

Ruthie clamped her fingers tightly around his hand and beseeched him with her eyes. *Stay. I'll cover you.*

He had no doubt she would pipe up and pray aloud in his place if they should go around the room adding individual praises and requests. But he couldn't do that. Couldn't be a hypocrite and stand here while everyone assumed he still bought in to their beliefs.

"I'll start," Pop said, perhaps to take attention away from the preacher and others staring at him as he stood there, mute and unmoving. "Dear heavenly Father, we thank You for—"

While all their heads were bowed, Gray pulled away from Ruthie's grasp and left the room.

* * *

Ruthie found Gray in the kitchen, feeding Cali a deviled egg that had been brought by one of Sobo's friends.

Gray didn't move to acknowledge her presence. Just leaned back against the counter, popped one of the paprika-sprinkled treats into his mouth, then wiped his lips with the back of his hand.

"One thing about those church ladies," he said, his gaze fixed on Cali, who eagerly awaited another bite of egg. "They sure know how to cook."

Ignoring the sour tone in his voice, she closed the distance between them and put her arms around him. He was hurting, and he clearly didn't know how to release it. She could turn her own cares over to God, but now that Gray had evicted God from his life, who did he have to turn to? His family? Their thoughts were currently focused on taking care of Sobo.

Her? She sighed. She didn't have the knowledge or training to help him through his pain. Knowing now what she did about the incident that had shaken his faith, she couldn't blame him for questioning why God hadn't saved the young man that Gray felt so responsible for.

"I know you only want what's best for Sobo," she said, and the words muffled against his shirt. She accepted that he was giving what he could. He had come over here tonight to check on his grandmother and help in whatever way he knew how. The group prayer had been too much, too soon.

Gray rubbed circles on her back with the palm of his hand. Although his touch was lazy and light, his arms felt stiff around her.

"It's okay," she continued. "Everyone knows you love her and want her to recover, too. You don't have to pray for me to know that about you."

As if he'd been holding himself together by mere force of will, Gray suddenly relaxed. "Thank you for that. It means a lot."

She stepped away and met his gaze. "Please tell me you didn't think I followed you in here to hit you over the head with a Bible." She frowned. "Did you?"

He moved away from the counter and started to pull the plastic wrap back over the eggs. Cali's watchful brown eyes followed his every move.

"The thought crossed my mind," he admitted with a sardonic laugh. "I'm sure my parents, uncle and the preacher gave it serious consideration."

Cali sat on her haunches, begging for the treat he carried to the refrigerator.

"Sorry, gal. Don't want you to get high cholesterol."

When the begging didn't work, Cali lowered her nose and covered her muzzle with her paws in the way she'd learned over the past week.

Gray stopped and held the refrigerator door open. His mouth slacked open, and he stared at the dog. "Don't tell me. You actually taught her to—"

"Savannah did," she admitted reluctantly. "She said if Cali could beg for food, she should also give thanks for it."

On hearing her name, Cali woofed and repeated the doggy prayer.

Gray twisted his mouth and stared down at the cute little beggar. "Sorry, girl. Prayers don't work."

Ruthie's heart tightened even as his expression softened a little. He reached under the plastic wrap to retrieve another half egg to give her. "Consider this a coincidence."

The grateful dog accepted the treat, and Gray returned the rest of the eggs to the cold refrigerator.

This was going to be a long uphill battle.

Chapter Ten

Over the next couple of weeks, Gray's life seemed to fill with sunshine and roses. Okay, so he wasn't normally a gooey sentimentalist, but he sure liked the way his life was going right now. His life with Ruthie.

"After your grandmother is up and around again," Savannah said, "you should bring her and Mr. Bristow to a Sunset Blessings event."

Gray smiled and nodded his thanks. "I'm sure they'd like that."

Although he and Ruthie hadn't been able to talk Amaya Kagawa into changing her mind and selling them the doll, Sobo hadn't yet noticed its absence. There were still a couple of days left until the aunt's birthday, which meant that even though it was unlikely they'd ever get the doll back, there was still a fraction of a chance Mrs. Kagawa might change her mind. For that reason, he had suggested to Ruthie that they hold off breaking the news to Sobo until after the aunt's party.

"She's getting stronger every day and has even

started walking a few steps across the room with her walker.

"That's awesome."

He accompanied her to Milk & Honey, where Paisley added sliced peaches to a pitcher of iced tea.

On a less-than-sunshine-and-roses note, Paisley gave him an update regarding the camouflage-wearing prowler that had been spotted again in their neighborhood. "Cali's been on edge," she said. "Sometimes she goes to the back door or a window and whines."

Gray had no doubt that only made the humans in the house more antsy. Ruthie and her roommates were understandably nervous, and he had taken to driving by their house to check on them every time he was in the area.

"You have my number," he reminded the women. "Call me anytime anything seems unusual, even if you think you're overreacting." He had already given the same instruction to Ruthie, but he suspected she might be reluctant to call on him. With her roommates on board with calling him, she might be less concerned about bothering him with what seemed like small worries.

He picked up the pitchers of peach iced tea Paisley had made for tonight's Sunset Blessings event and carried them to the yard behind the Abundance shops where Ruthie, friends, neighbors and a couple of customers had gathered.

Savannah set down some potato salad she'd made and playfully poked him with her elbow. "I knew you'd come in handy around here," she teased. "With muscles like those, it would be a shame not to put them to work."

Just for fun, he flexed his arm. Savannah touched the back of her hand to her forehead and pretended to swoon, then dashed back to Milk & Honey to help bring out the rest of the goodies.

He had dreaded the reactions of Ruthie's friends to the news that they were back together as a couple. But Ruthie had insisted that everybody had been pulling for them all along, and it couldn't have been more true.

She'd invited him to dinner at her house, where it had been planned they would announce to her friends that they were back on again, even if their engagement wasn't. That would take some time, but for now, she clearly wanted the blessings of the friends whose opinions mattered so much to her.

They had asked questions, sure. And he had answered them all carefully, giving a shortened version of the incident that had shaken his faith and assuring them that his intentions toward Ruthie were not only honorable but filled with love.

After that he and Ruthie were the golden couple. Pop and Sobo couldn't have been happier. Same with his parents and sister. Soon he and Ruthie were spending time together almost every day, which also meant spending more time with the people in her life. They were melding their lives and friends together. Melding everything but church. He actually found he enjoyed this newfound social life. And he was glad Ruthie was upholding her end of the bargain, offering no pressure whatever.

Officer Worth rode up right on schedule, and Gray lifted his chin in acknowledgment, but he wasn't the one in the crowd that the mounted policeman was looking for. He grinned and turned to go back inside and see if his muscles were still in demand—and maybe steal a kiss from Ruthie, who had gone inside with Savannah for the napkins and forks—only to be stopped by a friendly but heavy-handed punch to his shoulder.

"Dude! The Classic Car Club is having a cruise-in at the Steak & Brake tomorrow night." Matt Springer owned the shop across the street and sold classic-auto supplies and memorabilia. He was the one who'd provided the security tape of the parking lot and identified the make and model of Mrs. Kagawa's car. "You want to come?"

Although Gray had gone to Springer's shop to ask about the woman who'd bought Sobo's doll, they'd bonded over their mutual fascination with her classic Mazda Coupe. He thought about the self-defense class he had arranged to teach Ruthie and her friends after work. "I've got something going on tomorrow evening. I might show up for a little while afterward, though."

"Cool. Maybe I'll see you there."

Yep, he definitely liked this new turn his life had taken. He had not had much of a social life for so long that he hadn't realized what he'd been missing. Hadn't realized he'd been craving what others enjoyed as normal. Most of all, he hadn't recognized that a portion of the ache he'd attributed to Jakey's death had actually been the result of Ruthie's absence.

Because of what had happened overseas, he had thought he would never fit in here again. With that one stupid letter he'd written to Ruthie, he had given up everything. He had expected never to have this charmed life back. Now he had everything. He had Ruthie. He had hope.

The back door burst open, and Ruthie and Savannah joined the rest of the crowd at the picnic table. He reached out and pulled Ruthie to him for the sunset blessing before the eating began.

Ruthie snuggled under Gray's arm and bowed her head while Paisley said grace. She'd never realized she could love a person this much. The love they'd experienced before, though rich and real, paled in comparison to what they had now.

For one, they were older. More seasoned. Though she hadn't realized it while they were going through their time apart, they had needed that time to grow emotionally. To learn how to handle this more mature relationship. What they'd had before had been fresh and tender, vulnerable to the lashings life would give them. This was different. It was so much more.

She peeked over at Gray, aware that he merely stared down at his shoes, but at least he was here. At least he cared enough to go through the motions. The basics were there to build upon.

Most of the basics. The only cloud on the horizon was Gray's refusal to return to God. She wanted to know with a certainty that it would happen. That he would remember why he had believed in God in the first place.

But what if he didn't remember? Not that he'd asked again, but would she marry him even if he never went back to his faith? Such a disparity would certainly affect their day-to-day lives. In fact, it already had. Although they had taken the subject of faith off the table for now, they sure tiptoed around whenever talk turned to the church members who delivered meals to his grandparents. And it felt stifling not to be able to discuss with him the fascinating tidbits she learned at Wednesday-night Bible study. Could Ruthie be content in a relationship where every conversation was filtered until devoid of all godly topics? And on a more practical level, how long could she continue saving important but off-limits topics to discuss with Savannah or one of the others?

Deep down in her heart, she wanted Gray to believe again. If their relationship was to survive, it had to happen.

At the self-defense lesson the next evening, Ruthie noticed that Daisy seemed more comfortable in Gray's presence than she had that first night. A big reason for that change might have been the time she'd spent with him over the past couple of weekends, helping him with some backlogged filing and data entry that the regular receptionist hadn't been able to get to.

"Y'all have gotta hear this," Daisy said.

The girl put her cell phone on speaker and queued up her voice mail. A man's voice introduced himself as the personnel manager at the local power company and said the department supervisor had been very impressed by her recent interview for the administrative assistant position at the company. He indicated he would like for her to start work the week after graduation and to please call him as soon as possible to discuss the salary, benefits and other details.

The room burst into applause and cheers, and everyone celebrated as if the accomplishment was their own. For in a way, it was. Ruthie wished they could have done even more to help, but Daisy's father was a proud man, and he had a hard time accepting their generosity.

"You deserve it," Gray said. "And the power company is fortunate to have such a hard worker coming on board."

Savannah's enthusiasm bubbled almost as high as Daisy's. "Honey, I hope you called that man back right away and told him you want at least ten percent more than he offered."

Daisy grinned. "I did, thanks to Gray's coaching. And I listed all the reasons why I was worth it." She pushed her hair behind her shoulder in a playful show of haughty victory. "It was a no-go for the extra ten percent, but after he looked over my school accomplishments again, he agreed to meet me in the middle for the salary."

After a few more minutes of congratulations and good wishes, the group's attention turned back to the reason for their gathering. Gray kept insisting that the best defense was a good escape. But just in case any of them found themselves in a position where they couldn't get away from someone intent on harming them, he demonstrated some moves that would allow a smaller person to take down a larger one.

Despite Paisley's initial reluctance to participate when they started more than two weeks ago, she had soon warmed up to the training and was actually becoming good at it. Nikki, being more athletic than the rest, proved the best at following through on the moves Gray showed them, and Savannah's giggles and jokes at her own missteps kept everyone else laughing. Daisy followed through on Gray's instructions with a hint of hero worship in her eyes.

Ruthie's performance was the worst. She kept getting distracted by the instructor. She certainly understood the appeal he held for her young friend. His confidence and positive encouragement compelled everyone to give him their full attention. Which she happily did.

Once again, Gray paired them up, and every so often he surprise attacked one of them in an attempt to drive home the point that they needed to stay aware of their surroundings and the people around them. On the occasions when someone attempted the takedown maneuver on their "attacker," none was able to best him. But he merely used the failed incident to drive home his awareness message and the importance of avoiding a confrontation in the first place or escaping rather than fighting back.

"You never know when the pedestrian on the sidewalk near you may turn and do something unexpected," he said. "Be prepared."

The rest of them left in Savannah's car to return Daisy to her father, then head back to their own homes. Ruthie had no idea where the father and daughter would sleep tonight, which made her ever more grateful for the job that awaited her young friend. Although she and her roommates had done everything they could within their limited means to help, the father's circumstances and pride prevented him from accepting their generosity. And even though they had offered to let Daisy sleep on their couch, she refused to leave her father. Ruthie prayed the pair would soon have an apartment of their own and that Daisy would never need to use the self-defense skills Gray had been teaching them.

Ruthie could have ridden home with the others, but

Gray had insisted on driving her despite the classic-car cruise-in he planned to attend later tonight. She appreciated that he wanted to draw out his time with her.

They were picking up their belongings to leave when Gray grabbed her purse from the end table and quickly turned toward her. Sensitized to his ongoing message to be constantly aware of the actions of others, she went into defense mode. A split second later, with the purse swinging toward her, she lunged to one side to escape.

Gray reacted with a speed she had never seen before. As if by reflex, he swept his leg toward hers. In the next fraction of a second, all she noticed was the intensity of his gaze. The fierce determination to stop her. If she had seen that expression on a stranger's face, she would have been frightened. But in that short flicker of time, the only emotion she could register was confusion. And in the next half flicker, his expression changed to one that matched her own puzzled reaction.

Her knees buckled under the unexpected action, and the momentum took her down like a sapling felled by Paul Bunyan. Unfortunately, she fell like a heavy oak, landing first on her thigh and hip, then feeling the jolt of the floor against her side and arm.

Winded, she stayed where she had fallen and totally forgot about the escape portion of the lesson. All she could think to do at the moment was to drag precious air into her lungs.

Gray rushed to her side, knelt down and pressed a big hand against her shoulder to keep her from trying to get up too soon. "Hold on a sec. Let's see if there are any injuries."

His eyes, filled with such intensity only a second before, now revealed wide black pupils that took in her physical condition and mirrored back to her a large dose of fear. Fear of himself. Of what he'd done to her, apparently without realizing it.

"I'm so sorry." He repeated the words over and over, as if they might somehow undo his reflexive action. "I went to hand you the purse, and when you jumped at me, I—"

He cut himself off and gently helped her up.

"It's okay," she assured him, her voice strangely small after having the air knocked out of her. "I misunderstood. I thought you were continuing the 'be prepared for anything' lesson."

When it became evident that she could move all her limbs without difficulty and stand unassisted, he let her go and backed away as if afraid he might accidentally do more damage.

She knew he hadn't meant any harm. His reaction had been purely instinctive, just as her own had been. The stricken look in his eyes told her he might have surprised himself even more than he'd surprised her.

"I'm fine," she insisted. "It was an accident. You would never hurt me."

His face crumpled, and his shoulders drooped. "I already have. But I won't ever hurt you again. Never. I promise." He opened his arms and took her into his warm embrace.

The circle of his arms felt so safe and secure, and the strength in them told her he would do everything in his power to keep her out of harm's way.

She leaned back in his arms and gazed up at his handsome face, creased with concern and gazing back at her with pure love.

If only she could change his mind about the prayer thing, she felt certain it would all work out just fine.

The cell phone in her purse rang, breaking them from their tender moment.

She picked up the needlepoint purse she'd bought at an estate auction and glanced at the caller ID. "Paisley, it's been ages since I've seen you," she teased. "What's up?"

She was aware of Gray studying her while she listened. His expression turned serious when her demeanor changed.

"Did you call the police?" she asked after Paisley filled her in on what was happening at the house.

As if his protector radar had been triggered, Gray moved closer. Their tender moment was over, and he was all business now. "What is it? What's going on?"

"Lock the doors and stay put," she said into the phone. "We'll be there in five minutes."

Car keys in hand, Gray had already opened the door for her and motioned her through.

"Cali's acting weird and keeps going to the back door," she explained on their sprint to the car. "Paisley doesn't see anything that warrants a call to the police, but she's nervous after our previous run-in with the prowler."

Gray seemed to relax a little. "Nah, the prowler has probably moved on to an easier place to break in. Maybe Cali heard another dog in the neighborhood," he suggested. "Or a siren in the distance."

She hoped that was all that had set the dog off, but she doubted Paisley would have called unless the behavior had been extremely odd. Nevertheless, they made the trip from Gray's office to the house in record time.

They arrived at the house as dusk settled into night. The electronic-eye porch light that Gray had installed shone brightly to light the way up the walk path, and she wondered whether Paisley had switched it on for them or if a movement in the yard prior to their arrival had activated the device.

They paused for a moment in the car, taking in the scene, but all they could see was the area of the yard lit up by the porch light.

"Give me a minute while I check it out," he said.

The curtain at the front-room window drew back, and Paisley and Savannah stood there squinting into the dark, their hands shading their eyes. Cali appeared beside them and pushed her nose to the glass pane.

Gray entered the gate and peered over into the adjoining yard, perhaps assuming that if the guy was stupid enough to come back to the same house he'd unsuccessfully prowled before, he might try to hide in the same bushes where he'd found him before. Gray turned to her and lifted a thumb to let her know the front yards on both sides of the divided house were clear.

She joined him, feeling safe despite Paisley's concern that someone might be lurking around the house. Having seen Gray's lightning-fast reflexes up close, she had no doubt he could handle whatever had piqued the dog's interest. Choosing not to dwell on the fact that the prowler might have a weapon, she followed Gray to the front steps.

From the side of the house came a grunt and the sound of something heavy falling to the ground. Cali abandoned the front window and went crazy barking, and Ruthie's heart pounded in response.

Gray eased away from her to investigate, leaving her with the chicken's choice of scaling the steps two at a time to take refuge inside, or the brave-and-maybe-stupid choice of staying close to him, though she clearly wouldn't be of much help. Instead, her feet opted for choice number three by planting themselves to the ground where she stood.

So much for her self-defense lessons.

He motioned for her to go inside and slowly rounded the corner of the house, his posture guarded as if to fend off an attack in case the unwanted visitor decided to become aggressive.

"Don't move!" he ordered. "Stay where you are."

From the side of the house, over the din of Cali's barking, came a man's voice. "Sir! Yes, sir!"

At the unexpected response, Gray's body relaxed a mere fraction, giving her hope that the person he'd found was harmless. He paused, taking in the situation, and squared his shoulders even than more normal.

"Advance for inspection," he said, his bearing that of a high-ranking military officer and his voice so commanding even Ruthie felt compelled to obey. Instead, she forced herself to remain right where she was, with Gray positioned between her and the interloper.

A shadowy figure stepped out from beside the porch and into the front yard, where the porch light illuminated a middle-aged man in camouflage fatigues and sneakers. He could have been much younger. It was hard to tell. His leathery face might have come from age, hard living or most likely both. Frizzy brown hair had been pulled back in a short ponytail, and a scruff of goatee sprouted beneath his lower lip, lending an air of wildness to his already disheveled appearance. And a portion of a tattoo meandered from under his sleeve over the back of his hand.

To her surprise, the man looked confused and scared. Apprehensive. Much as Cali had when Gray had found her and carried her into the house to tend to her wound. This guy appeared to be uninjured, and he didn't seem to be a threat, but something just didn't seem right about him.

The stranger snapped to attention and saluted. "Reporting for duty, sir."

By now Cali had quieted inside. Paisley and Savannah watched from the window, and Ruthie noted that Savannah was talking on the phone. They must have called the police after all, for which she was relieved. Paisley gestured for her to join them inside, but Ruthie didn't want to distract Gray or risk escalating what was turning out to be a weird situation.

Gray kept up the role-playing, his voice softer now but firm and authoritative. "At ease, soldier."

The man actually seemed relieved to be told what to do, as if the strain of deciding his next move had been too big of a burden for him.

"Yes, sir, Major, sir."

His response didn't sound quite right, but since she didn't know military protocol, she wasn't in a position to question it.

"What is your business here?"

Cali woofed, her bark less frantic now and more curious.

For the first time, the man took his eyes off Gray and looked toward the house. Her roommates stepped away from the window, and she wondered if she should have gone inside with them as Paisley had urged. The "soldier's" gaze remained fixed on the house, leading Ruthie to suspect he might either try to run off or force his way into the house.

"Soldier, I asked you a question," Gray demanded. "Speak up. Give me your report."

The man babbled something about the mission he was on and how he could speak with Gray about it only because he was a major. The man said he had come to retrieve classified documents from this encampment, referring to the house. The more he talked, the more confused he seemed to be, as if he had a hard time keeping the details of his fantasy straight.

"What division are you from?"

The man told him his name, Private Denton, his gaze repeatedly returning to the window. "Major, this is urgent. My partner was captured on our first mission to secure the documents and is being held hostage. You've got to let me attempt a rescue."

He made a move toward them, and she retreated toward the divider fence. With his attention fixed on the front door, it seemed that escaping to the supposed safety of the house would be the wrong move at the moment.

Visibly upset, the man kept repeating that he had to get to his partner. Had to bring his partner back.

At the guy's first twitch, Gray had poised himself for a hand-to-hand altercation. He spread his arms and held his hands low, leaving no doubt he could take the guy down if needed.

The intruder started toward the house, stopped himself and seemed to change his mind a couple more times.

"Halt!" Gray commanded, giving him the option of a peaceful end to this confrontation. "Stand down, soldier."

All military protocol thrown to the wind, the man rushed past, shouting, "Radar!"

The front door opened, and Cali emerged, ears forward and on high alert. The dog zoomed down the stairs toward the man, her paws barely touching the steps.

Still going full throttle, Cali launched herself at him.

Chapter Eleven

Cali slammed into him so hard they both hit the ground and rolled. The supposed army private shrieked and threw his arms around the dog. Concerned that the animal might hurt the addled man, Gray reached for the collar to pull Cali off of him.

That was when he noticed the man's tears. He was crying. Cali squirmed in his arms, licking his face and grunting happy little "ooh-ooh" sounds.

Blue strobe lights lit up the yard, heralding the arrival of two squad cars. Ruthie met the officers at the gate and quickly briefed them on what had happened.

"Radar," the man murmured into Cali's fur. "You knew I'd come back for you. Didn't you, girl?"

Gray hated to interrupt their reunion, but the police were here to take the man into custody. "Hey, buddy," he said. "It's time to go with these gentlemen. They're here to help you."

Denton—Gray doubted he was currently enlisted in the army—looked up at him as though he'd forgotten he was there. "What gentlemen? Why?"

"The officers need to debrief you," he said, playing along with the fantasy the man had acted out earlier.

Denton rose unsteadily to his feet, and Cali—now known as Radar—circled his legs as if to keep him from leaving her again. One of the officers assisted him into the car, and Cali trotted back to Ruthie.

Gray wished she had gone inside as soon as she had come home. Her presence had heightened the stakes, making him more nervous for her sake than the situation called for. He didn't know what he would have done if something bad had happened to her. Didn't want to think of it.

The officer took their names and asked a few questions. Ruthie, ever compassionate, insisted she had no desire to press charges against Denton. Savannah and Paisley, who had joined them in the yard, agreed.

"What about the dog?" Gray asked.

"We can take it to the shelter for a few days," the officer said. "Mr. Denton will need to be processed, and it might be a while before he gets straightened out. The shelter won't be able to house the dog indefinitely."

By now Cali circled the yard, trying to go with her owner. Gray could tell that Ruthie's soft heart wouldn't allow them to take the dog to the pound, even if only temporarily. Ruthie called the dog and grasped her collar to keep her out of the way.

"I'll watch out for her," Ruthie promised Denton, who peered at her from the back of the police car. "Radar can stay with me."

Denton looked between Gray and Ruthie, then reluctantly nodded his assent. "She likes bologna," he said. "And a knuckle rub between the shoulders."

Ruthie grasped the collar tighter to steady the wriggling dog. "I'll do that for her. She'll be well taken care of."

Gray had no doubt Ruthie would follow through with the requests, but he suspected she'd be more generous with the knuckle rubs than with the processed meat.

Satisfied that his duty to the dog had been done, Denton reluctantly eased back in the car.

That matter settled, Gray asked the officer, "What's going to happen to him now?"

"He'll be evaluated. Probably have his meds adjusted." He straightened the watch on his wrist. "Since you folks don't want to press charges, he'll probably be released to the supervision of his social worker once he's ready to return home."

As the police cars drove off, Ruthie and her friends waved goodbye to Denton. Ruthie even lifted Cali's front legs off the ground and waved one furry paw after the dog's buddy.

Gray shook his head. It was as if they had been plunked down in Mayberry in a rerun of *The Andy Griffith Show.*

He walked away from the cluster of friends and stopped at the far side of the yard. The guy's earnestness to get to his partner had nearly been Gray's undoing. He understood the urgency. The feeling of helplessness and panic at not being able to protect his charge.

Denton's "mission" to retrieve his canine partner had brought back his own futile attempt to rescue Jakey Rayner. At least Denton had seen to it that his partner had made it to safety. Gray wished he could say the same for himself.

He rested his hands on the points of the white picket fence. Maybe he could have protected Ruthie better, he thought, as he second-guessed his actions. Denton had seemed harmless enough, but who knew what could have happened if the man had taken advantage of an opening.

A sick feeling settled at the pit of his stomach. He had failed once, four years ago, and couldn't let himself fail again. Never. Especially not when it concerned Ruthie. He lifted his hands from the fence, aware of the pressure dents in his palms from leaning against the wooden pickets. Given the choice, he would gladly put himself between her and any danger. Would have offered himself in exchange for Jakey, but he hadn't been given the choice.

"Oh, my goodness! You were amazing!" Savannah hobbled over to him and squeezed his arm appreciatively.

Paisley joined them, followed closely by Ruthie and Cali. "Yes, indeed. Cali was quite frantic," she said. "Thank God you were here to calm that man down. You were brilliant."

"Gray is amazing," Savannah declared. "A knight in shining armor."

Fortunately, Ruthie refrained from turning the event into a medieval knighting ceremony. "Would you two mind taking Cali inside?"

The two women flashed glances at Ruthie. At her nod, they disappeared into the house.

Then she looped her hand through Gray's elbow. "Looks like it's my turn to rescue you," she said with a small laugh.

Just as she expected, he didn't laugh with her.

The last thing she wanted to do was to give Gray a reason to leave her again, but after what they'd both just witnessed, she couldn't just stand here and pretend it had been an ordinary turn of events.

"I agreed not to pressure you, and I've upheld my end of the bargain," she said. "But you have to admit the situation couldn't have been choreographed better than how it turned out. You were here...the right person for the situation at the right time, with all the right things to say."

He pushed his fingers into his hair, and it looked as though he might actually give it a strong tug. "It's coincidence, Ruthie. Why can't it be just a simple coincidence?"

He sounded tired. Perhaps tired of having this discussion with her, but maybe he was just tired of arguing it with himself.

Whatever the case, she couldn't just let it slide. Couldn't let "coincidence" be the last word on the subject. She had agreed not to pressure him, but she hadn't agreed to stifle her own thoughts and beliefs in subjugation to his.

Despite her frustration with his unwillingness to see the truth, she purposefully softened her tone and focused on her desire to understand where he was coming from. "How can you show such compassion and understanding of others, yet not see that God put *you*— of all people—in that man's path? He needed someone strong. Someone who understood how to lead him where he was supposed to go. You were that person, and I believe God put you here for him in that moment."

Now she found herself pushing her fingers through her hair in an action that mimicked his gesture of a moment ago. She lowered her hands and was surprised to discover she'd left her hair intact.

"You can't call that a coincidence," she added.

Gray's jaw jutted forward, and he stared down at her, his expression stoic and hard. "Maybe I shouldn't have called it a coincidence," he admitted.

Finally! At last they were getting somewhere.

His hand squeezed hers in a manner that didn't quite match his expression. Perhaps to convey that he understood where she was coming from? That he was open to the possibility that although Jakey Rayner's prayer had not been answered in the way they had wanted, God was present and active in their lives every day?

"Maybe," he said, his eyes softening as he looked down at her, "a better term would be *fluke, happenstance, luck,* or *twist of fate.* I'm sorry, but two unexpected circumstances happening at the same time does not imply causality."

Slowly he released her hands, and she felt as though her heart would break in two.

She had tried to do all the right things. Live by example. Step back and give him space. Bite her tongue to hold back even the most innocuous comments that might be taken the wrong way. She had tried to be respectful and understanding, yet it wasn't enough. And might never be enough.

Well, enough about him. What about her? Could she be with him if he didn't believe? If he never changed his heart? She had thought such a pairing might be possible, especially since they were compatible in so many other ways, but maybe this one major difference couldn't be reconciled after all.

"I'm going to skip the classic-car event tonight,"

he said as casually as if they had just been discussing what they'd eaten for dinner. "I've got to go to the office tomorrow morning and finish some work at the office with Daisy."

He bent and kissed her, but the gesture warmed her about as much as ice cream on a snowy day. Then he got into his car and waited for her to go inside and lock the door before he drove off.

Ruthie went straight to her room and didn't bother to turn on the light. She had promised she wouldn't try to change Gray, but that didn't mean she couldn't ask God to do some fine-tuning on his heart.

She knelt beside the bed and pressed her palms together. This was too big for her to handle. Who better to turn it over to than God? Cali pushed her nose under her elbow, and Ruthie looped her arm around the Lab's neck.

"After all," she told the dog, "if God could change Saul's heart and the hearts of kings, He can surely change Gray's."

And if that prayer wasn't answered in the way she hoped, she would have to change her own heart...and let him go.

The prowler's capture warranted a two-minute spot on the eleven-o'clock news in which the anchorman explained that the delusional man had been apprehended while searching for his dog. Then the fickle media moved on to a three-car accident in neighboring Henrico County.

By the next morning, Ruthie's attention had turned to creating a display on the back wall featuring Sobo's hats and some stylized heart-shaped wrought iron pieces. Hard and soft. Cold, wintry colors and warm textures. Opposites.

Back to that again. Last night she had fallen asleep wondering if she should just set her concerns aside and try to find a way to meet Gray in the middle. Wishing it was even possible to mesh a relationship around two such divergent beliefs. And while she was wondering about the future, what about children? Was it possible to raise a child with two differently believing parents and not have the little one grow up confused and searching, possibly in the wrong places?

The front door to the shops opened and closed several times, so she needed to hurry and finish this job before any customers needed her attention. She moved a beveled-glass picture frame and temporarily set it on a small round display table where it wouldn't get broken while she climbed up to arrange the pieces on the wall. With a knee hold on the waist-high storage cabinet along the back wall, she climbed up onto the surface to drape some beads over the decorations for a feminine and festive effect.

"I'll spot you." Savannah appeared beside the cabinet and held her arms up in preparation to catch her if she fell.

A customer with a two-year-old daughter in tow paused to watch. "Ruthie, please be careful. You're making me nervous."

Milena, a regular at Gleanings and especially at Milk & Honey, had become a mother a few months ago after a trip to China to adopt little June. Since then, her mothering tendencies had widened to encompass everyone in her path, whether young, old, friend or stranger.

When the new mom had first brought June to the shop to show her off, Ruthie's thoughts had gone immediately to the baby she and Gray might have had if they had stayed together. Would their child have had dark hair and warm-toned skin like Gray's? Would the genes from Sobo's lovely almond-shaped brown eyes have been passed along through Gray to the child, or would there have been a hint of Ruthie's hazel eyes and reddish hair in their blended traits?

Now that she and Gray were back together, albeit connected by a fraying thread, there was another thought to add to her futuristic musings. Would the child go to church with her and learn that red and yellow, black and white, we're all precious in His sight? Or would that child stay home on Sunday mornings and learn that God is a fairy tale and that you have to rely on your own strength to get by?

She moved to one side to straighten the gold-and-black hat with the asymmetric brim, and her foot slipped on a scrap of paper that had been left on top of the cabinet.

Savannah and Milena gasped as one. Little June, thinking it a joke, squealed with delight, then giggled in anticipation of her doing it again.

"Ruthie, please come down," Milena pleaded. "Let me help you."

"I'm fine," she insisted as she righted herself and nudged the paper off the cabinet to avoid a repeat performance. "You go ahead and shop around. Holler if you need me."

Milena grabbed June by the hand. "We'll go over there where we can't watch you."

"Speaking of needing you," Savannah said, her head

tipped back and arms outstretched as if fully expecting her to fall. "How is Mrs. Bristow? Is she back to climbing the rose trellis yet? Considering your monkey antics today, I'm beginning to think you and she may be more than honorary relatives."

The bell over the door jangled again. The sound of money, Savannah had called it. All of the Abundance entrepreneurs welcomed the Saturday surge of customers.

She gave Savannah a quick update on Sobo's health and filled her in on the unresolved situation with the doll. "The aunt's birthday party is today, so it looks like we're going to have to break the news about the doll to Sobo very soon." She started to bend down for the pile of bead necklaces at her feet, then thought better of it. "Would you mind handing me the purple beads?"

Sobo's recent health crisis had driven home the unwelcome reality that Ruthie's loved ones were getting older. Only God knew how much longer she would be able to enjoy their company, so she needed to make sure to spend plenty of quality time with them now. The Bristows—all of them—were her family. Without them, she would be as adrift as the day her mother died.

No, she couldn't bear the thought of losing her honorary grandparents.

"What about you and Gray?" Savannah persisted. "You two seem pretty happy together. Does that mean your faith issues have been resolved?"

Ruthie focused on straightening the items on the Peg-Board wall. She couldn't bring herself to look at her friend, who would surely be able to see the conflicted feelings in her eyes—the joy of being back together with the man she loved, tempered by the feeling they were incomplete without the faith that had once connected them on a very deep level.

"Progress is slow," she admitted. "He has his heart set against God, but I'm praying and believing he'll eventually turn around. Hoping for sooner rather than later."

It had to be soon if their relationship was to survive. The longer she waited for Gray to return to God, the harder it would be to let go if this proved to be an irreconcilable point between them.

Savannah fell silent, an unusual occurrence for her bubbly friend.

Finished with arranging the wall display, Ruthie turned to ease herself down from the cabinet and found Savannah staring at a stern-faced Gray.

"That's not what we agreed," he said, his voice grim.

Savannah looked as if she'd rather be anywhere but here, but being the true friend that she was, she stayed and extended a hand to Ruthie. "Here, let me help you down."

"No," Gray intoned. "*I'll* let her down."

If Ruthie hadn't otherwise been focused on coming up with an explanation for her overheard comment, she might have taken a moment to mull over his odd choice of words.

Savannah scurried off and glanced over her shoulder at Ruthie, an expression of apology on her face for bailing out and leaving her to deal with Gray's dark mood alone.

Gray lifted a hand, and Ruthie reluctantly accepted the help he offered and gingerly clambered down.

He closed his fingers around her hand and grasped her elbow to steady her. Holding her this close made him want to pull her into his arms. But to do so would sacrifice his integrity. His sense of honor. The request to keep faith off the table had been a sincere one, and her comment to Savannah told him she hadn't taken it seriously, that she had merely been biding her time until he changed his mind.

Why did she have to go and ruin everything just when he thought they were doing so well?

Ruthie looked up at him with big eyes. She reminded him of the time when, as a teenager learning to drive, she had accidentally bumped her car into his in a clumsy attempt to parallel park. She had clearly been scared he would blow up at her for having dinged his precious Miata. But he hadn't then. Definitely wouldn't now either, even though she had dinged something even more precious than a car fender.

His trust.

The situation with Jake Rayner had taught him he couldn't count on God or anyone else to take care of him and the people he cared about. People had to take care of themselves. Right now he needed to protect himself from her unreasonable expectations.

What hurt most was Ruthie's unspoken message that he wasn't enough. That he would only be good enough if he would just ignore the life lesson he had learned in Afghanistan and come around to her way of thinking. But he couldn't ignore the fact that his friend was dead because Ruthie's God had ignored the kid's pleas.

Maybe he wasn't enough. If so, he was sure to disappoint Ruthie at every turn. What kind of a relationship was that? In addition to protecting himself, he needed to do the right thing and protect her from endless disappointments that would surely arise when he couldn't—and wouldn't—become the kind of person she wanted him to be.

He directed her to a quiet corner, away from the customer who studied an assortment of decorative wall clocks. In backing up, he bumped against a small display table, and he felt more than heard something wobble and fall. A millisecond later the brittle sound of broken glass filled the air.

He turned and stared down at an ornate picture frame that had split into four jagged pieces, then bent to pick up the sharp fragments.

"Don't worry about it," Ruthie said, touching a hand to his arm.

He yanked away from her. "You don't understand. I *do* worry about it." He scooped up the pieces and piled them on the cabinet where she'd been standing a moment earlier. "That's me," he said, pointing to the shards of glass and bent silver frame. "The frame can't be fixed, and God and your prayers can't fix me, either."

He gripped her by the upper arms, and she seemed so small in his hands. Her eyes had reddened, and she blinked back the moisture that threatened to spill over. Oddly enough, they didn't seem to be tears of remorse for having broken their pact but rather of disappointment. In him.

"I really wasn't trying to fix you," she said, her gaze pleading with him to understand.

That was the problem. He didn't understand. Didn't understand why a young soldier had to die, nor did he understand why she persisted in believing a fable. Why she expected that he should believe it, too.

"I just thought that—"

"That I would become what you want me to be? That I'm not enough just as I am?" He thought of the church hymn that promised he would be accepted just as he already was. What a cruel joke.

But it was no more cruel than staying in a relationship that defined him by what he wasn't. By the person he could never be again.

"I can't be the person you want me to be." He reached for Ruthie, but she pushed his hand away.

She squared her shoulders and stood as tall as she could in his looming presence. All this time, she'd been wishing, hoping, dreaming and praying that they'd overcome the one obstacle that kept them apart. She had hated when their relationship had broken up while he'd been at war, and now she hated that their recently renewed relationship had become a war front in its own right.

She wanted him to believe as she did, but he just couldn't do it. As long as they were together, this would be a point of contention between them, no matter how they bargained to abide by the status quo.

With a note of heartbreaking finality, she summoned from deep inside herself the courage to tell him, "I can't be with you and not want you to know and love God as I do. And I refuse to continue to cling to what I now know is false hope."

She felt the heat of Gray staring down at her. She bit down on her lips, which puckered from an attempt to hold back the sob that caught in her throat but which might otherwise look as if she were begging to be kissed. She'd done enough begging and conceding. Now was the time to hold firm, not only to her faith beliefs, but to what she wanted in a romantic partner and possible future mate. Even if it meant letting go. As much as she wanted otherwise, this relationship—this man—was obviously not meant for her.

Her chin trembled, and she regretted that he saw her weakness. Hoped he wouldn't read the sign of emotion as mixed feelings or, worse, uncertainty over what she was about to say.

"You were right the first time," she told him, her voice stronger than the spaghetti noodles that suddenly inhabited her bones. "This can't possibly work between us."

Gray pushed a hand through his hair. Despite his initial anger over her refusal to give up on her hopes of converting him back to being a believer again, he had not expected she would use this IED to resolve their differing stands. The sob that she'd been trying so valiantly to hold back now lodged itself in his heart. Her chin quivered again, making her seem small and delicate.

Delicate, yes, but he knew from experience that she could set her jaw in stubborn determination when she wanted something strongly enough. Although he wouldn't—couldn't—change his heart to appease her, he had no desire to throw away all the other things that had been going so well between them.

"Let's talk," he said, and tried to steer her toward the shop's exit. "You'll close Gleanings, and we can go over to Pizza Piazza for lunch. We can order breadsticks. Like old times," he urged, and belatedly realized he was using food to bargain with her. "Let's not be hasty. We can work this out."

She shook her head. "I'm not hungry," she said, letting him know without saying so that she would not budge from her stance.

These weren't old times, and what had worked for them in the past no longer brought them to a common ground.

The customer at the wall clock display lifted one from the shelf and tilted it in Ruthie's direction to get her attention. Both hands on the clock pointed straight up.

Ignoring the woman, she finished what she had to say. "I'm sorry, Gray, but this isn't working. It's better we end it now."

Now it was his turn to struggle to hold back the emotion. He tried not to notice her reaction. Eyes unnaturally wide. Biting her lip. Trying desperately to keep from crying. Any other time, his instinct to protect and comfort her would have compelled him to take her in his arms and hold her until all was well again. Unfortunately, all would never be well between them again. Their happy little experiment to coexist with opposing mind-sets had failed.

He pulled some bills from his pocket and left them on the cabinet to pay for the broken frame. Bent and shattered. That was exactly how he felt.

"I'll see you around at Sobo and Pop's," he said, and turned toward the door.

Ruthie watched in silence as he paused to pick up a small shard of glass from the floor.

Seeing her opportunity, and apparently oblivious to what had just transpired between her and Gray, the nearby customer hustled toward Ruthie, clutching a weathered Allentown clock to her chest as if a greedy shopper might snatch it from her.

"Are these all the clocks you have? I was looking for something similar to this one but a little bigger and maybe a different color." The woman held it out at arm's length and seemed to consider the possibilities. "I suppose I could paint this one. Maybe change out the hands for an antique spoon and fork."

Gray rose to his feet, clearly as dumbfounded as she was that anyone would consider altering such a great-looking clock.

Ruthie looked from the woman to the timepiece, finally settling her gaze on the open design of the large meshed gears and Roman numerals. Still reeling from their breakup, this one at her hands, she was so shocked by the outrageous question that it took a moment to form the words to reply.

Gray set the final shard of glass on the pile with the others. He was right—their relationship was as irreparably broken as the bits of glass that lay in front of her. In his mind it was broken because she wanted God in it. But she knew that for herself, any pairing without God in it was destined to come apart.

"If you change the clock, you'll ruin the patina," she told the customer, but her gaze never left Gray's face. "In this case, it's best to leave it alone and just appreciate it for what it really is."

Chapter Twelve

Ruthie's dream that God would change Gray's heart had been crushed. The truth was that his heart had indeed changed.

It had hardened even more than ever.

The Dear Jane letter had hurt so much that she'd thought she would never heal. She had thought nothing could be worse than reading that the man she loved more than anyone on earth wanted nothing more to do with her. Yes, that had hurt, but to be the one who broke up with him—in person—was much, much worse.

Four years ago, she had somehow managed to distract herself from the heartbreak by immersing herself in opening Gleanings and focusing on turning it into a success. Back then it had worked for brief periods of time, so today she attempted once again to stay too busy to think. Unfortunately, business slacked off for a little while after lunch, and Savannah had started puttering with the wedding dress. Her friend, on realizing the pain it caused her to look at it, had started to tuck it away, but Ruthie had insisted Savannah shouldn't alter her work schedule on her behalf.

Ruthie turned away from the sight. For the next couple of hours, she threw herself into her shop duties and hovered over customers in an attempt to erase the words that echoed in her brain: *It's better we end it now.*

For as little as she had accomplished this afternoon, she should have gone home. The distraction wasn't working.

What weighed heaviest on her soul was not only the fact that she had given up on Gray...but worse, that he had given up on God. Permanently.

Savannah ambled over from Connecting Threads. "Ruthie, honey, is there anything I can do? I just hate seeing you looking this miserable."

Ruthie looked up from her paperwork and wondered inanely if Gray and Daisy were still going over his security company's paperwork. She met her friend's compassionate gaze. Today Savannah wore a vintage wrap dress that she had refashioned with embroidered embellishments over the bodice and a sheer flowy skirt to cover the bottom. This modernized version looked very little like the original and very much like Savannah. Ruthie's attention dropped to the long fluff of white fabric draped over her arm.

Following her gaze, Savannah looked down, appeared to realize what she'd done and belatedly moved the veil behind her back.

Ruthie's jaw hurt. Probably from clenching her teeth. At least it diverted her attention from other, deeper hurts. "Thanks, but there's nothing you can do. Nothing anyone can do."

That was the part that hurt the worst. She could handle disappointments that came along in life as long as there was a plan, something she could do to make it right again. The day between learning that her step-father was going back to New Jersey without her and receiving Sobo and Pop's insistent invitation to come live with them had felt like a bottomless chasm. But the plan to move in with the generous couple—people she barely knew—had given her hope. A lifeline just when she'd needed it most.

For the past couple of weeks, she'd had such a lifeline with Gray. True, she had agreed not to try to coerce him into changing his mind, but her private plan had been to wait him out in hopes he would eventually see the calm assurance and the sense of peace he'd been miss-ing without God in his life. But that lifeline had been steadily unraveling until, today, it had finally broken.

So she had to come up with a new plan. A plan to accept this new turn of events and trust that God would protect Gray and ultimately—perhaps even years from now—lead him back to church and the faith that had previously been such an important part of his life. The acceptance part was so hard, especially when it meant not having Gray in her life. So she needed to come up with an additional plan. One that would fill the gap-ing void in her heart. Staying busy at work helped only to a point.

"Actually, there is something you can do," she told Savannah. "Let me know if any customers need me. I'm going over to Milk & Honey for some hot tea and to try to figure out what comes next."

Ruthie examined the menu while she mulled over her next move. Sobo always said that whenever you need something, give it away to someone else. Well, today she was sad, so the obvious solution would be to cheer up someone else.

She started a list while waiting for Paisley to take her order. Help the homeless, as Paisley did? Follow Savannah's lead and volunteer at the children's adoption agency? Perhaps offer to help out at the animal shelter where Cali—Radar—had almost been sent? Or go visit Private Denton at the VA hospital?

She drew a heavy line through the last possibility. Mainly because Denton might not be ready for visitors at this point, assuming he wanted any, but also because interacting with military veterans would remind her of the very person she was trying so hard not to think about.

Paisley draped a bar towel over her shoulder and swaggered over to the table as if she were a bartender in an old Western. "What's your poison, pardner?"

Ruthie smiled, glad for her friend who always knew just how to lift her spirits. "Earl Grey," she said. "Straight up."

Paisley returned a few minutes later and set the tea and a scone in front of her. Then she took a quick look around to see if anyone needed her before seating herself at the table. "I was so chuffed about you and Gray getting back together. I thought for sure it would work out this time."

Ruthie took a careful sip of the hot tea, then shook her head. "I should have known it wouldn't work. Unequally yoked and all that," she said, repeating the reason Gray had cited in his original breakup. "But I was so sure God intended for us to be together."

She still felt that the verse from Jeremiah had been a message for her. *Plans to give you hope and a future.*

Maybe she had misunderstood, and God had planned to give her hope and a future with someone else.

The very thought made her stomach churn.

"You'll get through this," Paisley assured her.

Unfortunately, Ruthie had no idea how. Since her friend was in a listening mood, she poured her heart out, starting with her initial determination to give her relationship with Gray another go even though he was still adamantly set against the faith that was such an important part of her own life.

"To make matters worse," she continued, "today is the day of the birthday party for Mrs. Kagawa's aunt. I'm going to have to tell Sobo that I accidentally sold her doll. It'll break her heart." Since she was already riding the pity train, she poured out the other piece that had been weighing at the back of her mind. "And after Mr. Denton gets his meds straightened out, I'll have to say goodbye to Cali."

Although she knew Cali—rather, Radar—loved her owner and belonged with him despite his troubles, having to give up the sweet dog was the final straw that threatened to break her emotional back. Her eyes filled with tears of sadness and loss, and the sunshine that poured through the café window seemed to mock her with its good cheer. She shook out her napkin and dabbed her eyes.

Paisley had rested a sympathetic hand on her arm, but her attention was focused beyond Ruthie on something outside the window. "Somebody's running across the parking area." The bell over the door jangled at the abrupt entry. "And I think she's looking for you."

Ruthie turned in her seat and took in the well-dressed woman who paced the front of the shop and looked around frantically. The customer's words tumbled out so fast it was hard to understand her, and she seemed very agitated.

Mrs. Kagawa.

"What now?" Ruthie muttered. Was the customer upset because she'd found a defect on the doll? That would be just her luck.

Determined not to follow Gray's lead, she pushed the thought of luck away from her mind. Whatever was going on, good or bad, she asked that God use the situation in a way that would bless them and honor Him.

Mrs. Kagawa noticed her and spun in her direction, and she covered the distance with amazing quickness.

Ruthie rose to her feet and mentally braced herself for whatever was to come. She didn't know what was going on, but she had a sickening feeling she was about to be hit with more bad news.

Speaking even faster than before, Mrs. Kagawa stopped at the table and tumbled the words out in what sounded like a haphazard fashion. Although Ruthie couldn't make out exactly what the problem was, there was no question the woman was in supreme distress.

Paisley stood and pulled out a chair for their visitor. "Slow down. Take a breath," she urged. "Have some tea."

"No time," said Mrs. Kagawa. "*Obasan* open present and see doll. Now she cry, and she cry more. No stopping. She only say, 'Whose doll?' I don't know what is matter."

Ruthie didn't know whether to comfort her or probe for answers. She finally settled on asking a couple questions of her own. "Why are you telling me this?" she asked softly. "What do you want me to do?"

"You come," Mrs. Kagawa said, holding out a hand for her to follow. "You tell her about doll. She stop cry." She reached for Ruthie and tugged at her sleeve. "Come, quick-quick."

Until Gray had come into the shop looking for the doll less than a month ago, she had never paid much attention to it where it had sat on a shelf at the Bristows' house. For that reason, she doubted she could answer the aunt's questions about it, nor could she offer any comfort that the aunt's own family hadn't already attempted to provide.

Gray knew more about the doll than she did. Maybe he could help shed light on this strange turn of events. On the way out, she reached for her cell phone and hit the speed-dial button that connected her to Gray.

"Meet me at Mrs. Kagawa's house. Something's going on with the doll."

The inside of the Kagawa house was even more beautiful than the outside. The minimalist decor combined clean Japanese lines with comfortable American furniture that made Ruthie feel both welcomed and a little in awe of the careful styling.

At the front of the room, an older woman took the place of honor in a plush wingback chair that nearly swallowed her tiny frame. The matriarch's dark hair, almond eyes and amber skin were echoed in the family members clustered around the room. A couple of children stared openly at Ruthie.

The aunt's face was splotchy from crying, and tears glistened on her lashes. In her lap sat two identical dolls, one dressed in royal blue and the other—Sobo's—in red.

Mrs. Kagawa introduced her aunt as Tomiko Kishimoto and explained that she had purchased Sobo's doll because it was a perfect match to the one Tomiko already owned. She said something in Japanese to her aunt, and the elderly woman teared up again. Clearly confounded by the predicament, Mrs. Kagawa turned to Ruthie, her expression one of helpless frustration.

"See? She crying."

Ruthie went to the aunt and offered a bow of respect. *"Kon'nichiwa."* Thank goodness she remembered the basic greetings Sobo had taught her more than ten years ago. *"Watashi no namae wa* Ruthie *desu."*

The woman looked at her and politely dipped her head.

Taking the gesture as one of acceptance, she knelt to interact with the woman at her level.

Mrs. Kishimoto said something in Japanese, but her speech was much too fast and too advanced for Ruthie to follow. She turned to Mrs. Kagawa in a silent request for her to translate, but the elderly aunt grabbed her arm and gripped it tightly. Taken by surprise, she could only marvel that someone so tiny could clamp on so hard.

One of the children, a boy about three or four years old, sidled closer to Ruthie. Slowly, almost reverently, he lifted a hand and touched her hair so lightly she barely felt it.

Mrs. Kagawa spoke to the boy in Japanese, her face and tone stern, and he stepped away. To Ruthie she said, *"Oba* wants to know where you found the doll."

Ruthie directed her answer to the aunt. To reply in Japanese was beyond her ability, so she mimed in conjunction with her response. Pointing a finger at her own chest, she said, "My *sobo*."

Apparently surprised at her use of the Japanese word for her relative, the woman jerked her gaze to Ruthie's red hair.

Understanding the matron's confusion over a Japanese woman having produced a granddaughter with red hair and fair skin, she quickly explained, "Sobo is my honorary grandmother. I love her the same."

Mrs. Kagawa translated. The aunt leaned forward in the chair and gently touched Ruthie's face.

Surprised by the unexpected gesture, Ruthie sat and accepted what could only be described as a loving touch. She became aware of the door opening and someone entering the room. Gray must have arrived. If her chin hadn't been so carefully cradled in the aunt's thin fingers, she might have turned to see him. See if the hurt he wore earlier today was still evident on his face. Or had he forgiven her for breaking up with him? Breaking both of their hearts.

The woman turned the dolls toward her and lifted the red dress to show her the Japanese characters that had been handwritten on its leg. Sobo's doll.

"*Imōto-san*. Naoko." Tomiko pointed to Ruthie and added, *"Obaasan."*

Yes, Naoko was her *obaasan*. Her grandmother, of sorts. She had known without the extra hint that the red-dressed doll belonged to Sobo and wondered what she was getting at. And what did *imōto-san* mean?

Gray cleared his throat and introduced himself in Japanese as Naoko's grandson.

The woman's gaze left her face and turned toward

him, her face lighting with delight. *"Oi,"* she said. She bowed her head, then again. *"Oi."*

Gray blinked in response, apparently taking in what she said.

Mrs. Kishimoto urged him to pull up a chair beside her, then showed him the writing on the other doll, in the same location.

"Onē-san," she said, and in a gesture mimicking Ruthie's earlier one, pointed to herself and added, "Tomiko."

Mrs. Kagawa gasped, and the others in the room all fell silent.

Ruthie recognized the name Tomiko from their introduction and assumed she was indicating the doll in the blue dress belonged to her. The dolls' resemblance and the fact that they sported similar writings left her wondering where this conversation was heading. Did she and Sobo know one another? One look at Gray, and the reaction of the others, told her they understood exactly what was going on.

The birthday lady reached over and patted Gray's hand in a show of familiarity and affection. *"Oi,"* she repeated.

Apparently stunned by the revelation, he sat back in the chair to take it all in.

"What?" Ruthie asked. "What is it?"

He turned his gaze to her. *"Imōto-san* means little sister," he said. *"Onē-san* is big sister." He frowned, deep in thought. "I thought Sobo was an only child."

Ruthie leaned back from her kneeling position and thumped to a resounding sit. Tomiko Kishimoto was Sobo's big sister. With that bit of information in place, she now recalled the other family word Sobo had taught her. *Oi*. Nephew. This sweet elderly woman was Gray's great-aunt. It took a moment for everything to sink in. The odds of their encountering each other an ocean and several decades away were astronomical.

Gray leaned back, processing this groundbreaking information. He met Ruthie's gaze, and she wished she could offer him the kind of comfort and assurance she would have liked for herself right now. But this moment was not about her and him.

Mrs. Kishimoto, having overcome her earlier distress, now excitedly told the story of how she had come to have this doll, and her niece translated for her.

As young children living outside of Tokyo, the girls had been given identical dolls. Although their mother had made different-colored dresses for them, the sisters had marked the dolls to prevent their getting mixed up. Naoko often slept with hers at night to calm her fears of the dark.

All the others—Gray's new family members, and hers by association—were as enthralled as she at hearing the story of two sisters growing up a world away and so many decades ago.

Tomiko fast-forwarded into the story about ten years. When Naoko was only sixteen, she answered an ad for employment at an office in nearby Tokyo. Anxious about going for her first job interview, she had tucked the doll in her bag to calm her nerves. Tomiko and the family had kissed her and wished her well, then sent her on her way.

Mrs. Kagawa, apparently also hearing this for the first time, continued translating. Her voice grew soft. "A terrible thing happen that day," she said. "Naoko never come home."

The family had wondered why she had not contacted them and had feared she'd been badly injured. Tomiko had been looking for her ever since, guided to the United States by a witness who saw an American serviceman—Pop?—rescue Naoko from a vicious mugging. Having learned the serviceman's company was originally from Virginia, Tomiko had eventually moved here in hopes of locating that man and finding out what had become of her sister.

Ruthie glanced over at Gray, who was visibly shaken by what he heard. To the young people in the room, this was a fascinating story about a stranger they'd never met. But to Gray it was a piece of his grandmother's personal history. She felt certain his heart must ache at the thought of Sobo, a vulnerable young girl alone in the city, being attacked by a stranger.

He was so close, almost close enough to touch, but seemed so far away. She wanted to take his hand and let him know he wasn't alone. Wanted to let him lean on her, but she couldn't.

Tomiko reached for him, her demeanor cautious, and asked a question.

"She want to know," Mrs. Kagawa said, "if Naoko still alive."

Gray stood and bowed to his newfound great-aunt. "She's very much alive," he said, and briefly explained that she was currently recovering from a broken hip. "I'm sure she would be honored to see you." Then he turned to Mrs. Kagawa, gave her his grandparents' address and asked her to bring Tomiko and meet him there in thirty minutes.

Ruthie rose and stood on the periphery of the circle that now clustered around Gray. She was not officially connected to these nice people who were Gray's new family, but neither was she a total bystander.

He looked to her and nodded toward the door. "Want to ride with me? I'm sure Sobo and Pop will want you there."

Her role in joining him today was not as his partner, but as Sobo's grandchild.

Gray stuck his head in Sobo's room and found Pop reading a home-repair magazine while his wife napped. He beckoned his grandfather into the living room, where he broke the news about Sobo's doll and the history behind it. Ruthie filled in the bits that he left out, and he was glad to have her here. Her calm presence and softly spoken words provided a positive perspective in the midst of their whirlwind discovery.

Pop sat between them on the sofa and pushed shaky fingers through his white hair.

Ruthie was the first to break the weird silence that ensued. "Sobo never spoke of her sister. Did they have a falling-out?"

That possibility had never occurred to Gray. Now he wondered if he'd done the right thing by inviting Tomiko and her family to meet Sobo.

Pop looked up, his gaze far away as if he was remembering what had happened so many years ago. "Naoko was never able to tell you about her past, because she didn't remember it. She has amnesia."

The mugging. It must have been bad if it had left her with a head injury that blotted out her entire childhood.

"It was during the Korean War. She had been lured with the prospect of a job in Tokyo. The pay was more than most receptionist jobs offered, which should have been a tip-off, but what young woman wouldn't have been excited about making a lot of money for her first real job?" He looked toward the hall, listening for Sobo's call, then lowered his voice. "She was abducted and beaten, presumably by the man who had placed the ad. I happened to be on R & R that weekend and saw a pretty young woman getting roughed up by a guy who was trying to push her into his car. Other than shouting for help, people stood around watching, but nobody did anything about it. Probably too shocked to react, or maybe they were afraid they'd get hurt if they tried to help her."

He and Ruthie had already heard this part of the story, but she drew in a sharp breath as if it were the first telling. He didn't blame her. Tomiko had glossed over the details, or perhaps her niece had left them out during translation. At any rate, Pop's blow-by-blow rendition was hard to hear.

"I gave him a taste of his own medicine," Pop said, modestly diminishing his role in the event, "but by the time I reached them, he had already beat her pretty bad. Knocked her unconscious. I didn't wait for an ambulance. Just picked her up and carried her to the hospital two blocks away and stayed with her for the rest of my R & R."

Ruthie had pressed her knuckles to her mouth. "Thank God you were there at the right place and right time. And that you were willing to risk your own safety to help her."

He understood why his grandfather had done it. The need to protect others must have been in Pop's DNA, passed down to Gray's father and then to him.

"She was treated for a head injury, but the doctors

couldn't help with her memory loss. We were told that if it didn't come back after a few months, it would probably be permanent. And it was. The doctor said if she got another concussion, it could cause more serious problems. Even life threatening."

Ruthie moved closer to Pop to lay a comforting hand on his arm, and he pulled her to him to kiss her lightly on the forehead. "What about her attacker?" she asked. "Was he ever found?"

Pop shook his head. "He drove away before anyone could get a look at his license plate. The police were able to figure out from the classified ad found in Naoko's pocket that she'd been the latest target of a human-trafficking ring."

It sickened Gray to think what might have happened to Sobo if his grandfather had stood back like everyone else and watched without acting.

"She also had the doll with her, but it didn't offer any clues," Pop said.

Ruthie rose and paced the floor. "But it said 'little sister' on the doll. Didn't that give a clue that she had family?"

Pop rubbed a hand across the afternoon crop of white whiskers on his cheek, and the raspy sound matched his voice. "She insisted it meant the doll was 'Naoko's little sister.' We assumed a quirk in her brain had allowed her to remember that piece of information even though everything else was locked away. But she must have made an assumption and latched on to it as fact."

Knowing now what he did about his grandmother's head injury, it was easy to see why Pop had worried so much about her hitting her head when she fell off the rose trellis.

The rest was the stuff of Hollywood movies. Pop went on to explain that he visited her in the hospital and later in rehab whenever he could get approval to return to Tokyo. And in between they wrote letters. They fell in love, and when it was time for her release from medical care, she became his war bride and went on to create a lifetime of happy new memories with him.

Gray hoped that someday he would find someone to create happy memories with him. A surreptitious glance over at Ruthie caught her watching him just as she used to do at the piano, and he quickly jerked his gaze back to his grandfather. He had thought Ruthie was the one, and they'd made a good start at creating happy memories, but it wasn't meant to be. Too much murky water under that bridge.

Sobo's sleep-groggy voice drifted to them from the other room.

Aware now of the delicate medical condition Sobo had kept so well hidden all these years, Gray wondered again if he'd made a mistake in inviting Tomiko here today. "Do you think Sobo can handle the shock of meeting her sister after so much time has passed?"

Pop paused at the door and considered his answer. "I suppose we should let her make that decision."

He and Ruthie followed their patriarch down the hall to Sobo's room, where she greeted them with her usual delight to see them.

As they entered the room, he caught Ruthie making an emu hand for silent prayer. Perhaps, like him, she was hoping that hearing the story about Tomiko would trigger Sobo's memory. Strangely, he found he wasn't annoyed by the ever-present sign of her faith.

He sat on the edge of the bed next to his grandmother. "Sobo, we have something very important to tell you."

Chapter Thirteen

Pop started off by telling Sobo about mistakenly taking the doll and his box of war memorabilia to Gleanings for Ruthie to sell. Ruthie, now absolved of guilt for having sold the doll thanks to the recent turn of events, admitted that it had been sold and explained their attempts to find the customer and retrieve it.

Gray noticed the look of anxious concern that crossed Sobo's face. "Don't worry," he quickly assured her. "It gets better."

Sobo smiled and reached for Ruthie, who clasped her hand. But instead of holding on, Sobo placed Ruthie's hand in his and patted them both. She didn't know he and Ruthie had broken up again.

Gray sighed. That was more news they needed to tell her. But not today. Let her enjoy the reunion with her sister. No need to tarnish her joy. Not yet.

He went on to explain about the birthday party for Mrs. Kagawa's aunt and the revelation that the woman now had two identical dolls.

Pop filled in the last, most pertinent bit of information. "You have a sister."

Gray didn't know what he had expected, but it certainly wasn't a curious tilt of her head and a blank expression. After all the final puzzle fragments had been pieced together today, he had assumed Sobo would look at the completed picture and recognize the image they had presented to her. Perhaps he had hoped her reaction would be even more excited than those of Tomiko and her family.

Pop looked crestfallen.

Ruthie pulled her hand from Gray's reluctant grasp and slid her arm around Pop's shoulders. "Give it some time. This is a lot to take in at once."

The doorbell rang, announcing the arrival of Sobo's sister. Sobo seemed anxious, and Gray wondered if this was too much to spring on her in one day. What if the reunion turned sour? Maybe they should have waited to let the information sink in for a few days before attempting an introduction. Unfortunately, that wasn't an option now. He only hoped their meeting again after all these years wouldn't do more harm than good.

"You don't have to meet Tomiko if you don't want to," Ruthie said, echoing his own thoughts.

Sobo forced a tentative smile. "I want."

He had always seen his grandmother as an active, lively person who could do anything she set her mind to. In her, he saw a physical strength, as well as mental fortitude. Now, for the first time, he saw an even deeper strength. A strength that had pushed aside self-pity over the loss of her memory and all the people in her past. A strength that had allowed her to trust the man who had rescued her to bring her to this new country with its unfamiliar customs, where he would love her and protect her.

He excused himself and welcomed Tomiko and her niece into the house. They had left the rest of the family behind so as not to overwhelm Sobo. He quickly briefed the women on Sobo's memory loss and warned them not to expect much of a response from her.

Tomiko clutched the dolls as if they were talismans that would see her safely through the relationship maze she was about to step into.

He led her into the room and offered her the recliner, but she stood beside the bed, transfixed, and gazed down at her sister. It was as if she was remembering the girl she had last seen and was running the image through a sixty-year time machine to see if it matched up with the person before her.

It apparently did. Tomiko abruptly sobbed and dabbed her swollen eyes with a wadded tissue. Her niece stood back and watched, making no effort to comfort her, since these were tears of joy.

Sobo stared back at her, clearly not registering the woman in front of her as the sister she had left behind. Gray's heart cracked, both for Sobo, who might never recover her lost memories, and for Tomiko, who had found her sister and understandably wanted all of her back.

Quietly, as if afraid of shattering the illusion, Tomiko spoke in Japanese. He didn't catch much except the word *chan,* an affectionate term for sister.

A moment later, something changed in Sobo's expression as a dawning awareness penetrated her fractured memory. Her lips parted to speak, but nothing came out. Then, finally, after a painfully long moment, "Miko?"

Tomiko nearly crumpled where she stood, and Gray

moved to catch her. But his assistance was unnecessary. Tomiko draped herself over her sister, and the two women hugged and cried. Then they pulled back, beamed lovingly at each other and hugged and cried some more.

Overwhelmed by the display of raw emotion, and even more by the sheer impossibility of what had just occurred, he moved to the door to let them catch up on their lost years.

Ruthie followed him out of the room, beaming and brushing away a tear with the heel of her hand. Obviously thrilled to have been a witness to the touching reunion, she reached for his arm.

Barely aware of her touch, he pulled away. A sense of stunned amazement fell over him like a numbing blanket that both shielded him from the painful joy of the long-awaited reunion and surrounded him with the knowledge that this couldn't have happened. Not like this. Not in a million years.

Unable to feel at the moment, let alone think, all he knew was that he had to get away from the heightened emotions that stirred his soul and the contradictions that challenged his thoughts.

He didn't know where he was going. Just let his feet carry him where they would through the unseasonably chilly day. The wind blew against him, urging him to go back. In defiance, he shoved his hands into his pockets, hunched his shoulders and pushed against the cold blast.

It should have been impossible for Sobo's sister—his great-aunt—to find her. The weirdest part was that he couldn't call this one a coincidence. As difficult as it was to admit, something deep down told him that mere coincidence could not have orchestrated events so Tomiko's search eventually led her to the passerby who had witnessed Sobo's rescue by the American soldier who was now his grandfather.

Despite his resistance over these past four years, he knew with a certainty that coincidence had not led Tomiko to Richmond, Virginia, where that soldier lived. Only God could have done that.

Wordlessly, he walked down the street and found himself at the church where all those he loved most came to worship.

Just as he had done three short weeks ago, he paused at the bottom of the steps to the welcoming portico. The chilly air swirled around him, questioning his actions. Slowly, cautiously, he ascended the stairs.

The door was unlocked. Gray pulled it open and stepped inside. Into the warmth.

Ruthie followed Gray to the church. Just as he had done a moment earlier, she paused at the steps. He had pushed her away before. He might do it again.

Never mind that. Gray was at church, and he hadn't been dragged here against his will. She said a silent prayer, asking God to guide him to the knowledge and understanding that he sought. "Lord, You helped Tomiko find her sister," she whispered. "Please help Gray find his way back to You."

She went inside and found him seated on the pew closest to the altar, elbows on knees and head resting in his hands. He looked...not defeated. Broken, maybe. It was hard seeing him like this. Seeing the man she had always viewed as big, strong and in control bent into a weary, overwhelmed posture. It was odd. And a little frightening.

She proceeded down the aisle to sit next to him. If he didn't want her there, he could send her away, but something told her he shouldn't be alone right now. He needed her.

She needed him.

She had almost reached the pew when he rose and walked to the altar. Slowly, he fell to his knees and bowed his head.

Unasked, she knelt beside him and assumed his posture. As she expected, he didn't respond. It didn't matter.

She slipped her hand into his, then wondered if she was pushing too hard. *Don't think,* she heard from somewhere deep within. *Just be.*

After a moment he pulled away. But this time he reached into his pocket and withdrew his wallet. From a small pocket inside the billfold, he took out a worn letter and unfolded it. Ruthie recognized the handwriting as her own.

Gray held it open in front of him, staring but not appearing to see what was written on the paper. Her handwriting filled the page. "This was the last letter you sent me before I…"

Before he broke up with her. She remembered copying the psalms and sending them to him to read whenever he needed comfort. But instead of comforting him, the verses had only served to point out the divide in their beliefs.

Had he come here to ball up that letter? To put the final finish to his relationships with both God and her?

At the top of the page was Psalm 20:1.

Gray blinked a couple of times as if to clear his vision, then read the verse aloud. "'May the Lord answer you when you are in distress. May the name of the God of Jacob protect you.'" Without looking at her, he cleared his throat. "Every time I saw that verse, it smacked me in the face. But for some reason, whenever I tried to throw this letter away, I couldn't do it."

The God of Jacob. Of Jakey. No wonder he had taken it so personally when his friend had died. That verse must have seemed as though it was mocking him.

"When Jakey and I were under fire, he called out to God to protect us," he said, reminding her of the painful events of that day. "To protect him, just like the verse promised."

She touched his arm. "You don't have to go through this again. I understand."

"No," he said, shaking his head. "You don't. Here's the part I didn't tell you."

She sat back on her heels and waited until he was ready to tell her the rest.

"Jakey prayed for protection, and at that exact moment he was hit by shrapnel. I was so busy trying to get us out of there, I hadn't even *started* to pray. Yet I was the one who was spared." He blew out a breath. "Explain that."

It was understandable that such a disaster had caused him to question God's presence. Her heart ached for him, and she wished there was something she could say to make sense of what was an incomprehensible tragedy. No wonder he had decided he couldn't count on God during the bad times and refused to give Him credit for the good. No wonder he attributed God's blessings to coincidence.

"There's no way I can explain what happened in Afghanistan. Only God knows those answers," she said. "But you have to admit that more than coincidence must have been at work to reunite Sobo with her long-lost sister. A sister she didn't even remember until today."

Gray nodded. "Yeah, that's pretty freaky." He smoothed out the letter and let his gaze roam over the verses. "After what happened today, it looks like maybe God was with us after all. Today and back then."

The impact of his words hit her like a velvet-covered brick. She almost dared not hope that his frozen heart had started to melt.

He spoke again, and this time his voice was stronger. Clearer. "A stray dog joined us when I was struggling to get Jakey back to camp. He showed up from out of nowhere...as though he was sent to protect us. More than once that mutt let us know when enemy soldiers were nearby." Gray turned toward her, and his gaze bored deeply into her eyes. "Here's the weird thing. I named that dog Radar. Was that a coincidence?"

There was no sarcasm to his question. Only a sincere earnestness as he sorted through the evidence of God's presence that had been there all along...evidence that he'd been unable to see at the time.

"You know what I think," she said.

He sat silent for a moment, apparently taking it all in as he stared at the letter. "There were other verses. Promises of hiding places and songs of deliverance. At the time it seemed like those promises hadn't been kept, but now I wonder." He rubbed a hand over the back of his neck. "The shelter we needed always showed up at just the right time. And then there was the time I lost my way back to the unit." He shook his head as if barely able to comprehend how he hadn't seen this before. "Just when I thought I'd never find my way back, songs from a wedding in a nearby village helped me regain my direction."

Coincidence, indeed. Ruthie leaned closer to him, feeling the warmth of his arm against her shoulder, and her gaze fell on another verse: "I will strengthen you, though you have not acknowledged me."

"You hadn't acknowledged God," she said. "But He gave you the strength to carry through anyway." She laid her hand on his. "God's hand had been on you the entire time."

He turned his hand upward and captured her fingers with his. "I just wish Jakey hadn't died."

She squeezed back. "Me, too."

Perhaps they would never understand why the faithful man had had to die so young. For now, it would have to be enough to trust that Jakey was safe in God's heavenly embrace.

Gray rose to his feet and held out a hand to help her up. "My sweet, loyal Ruthie." He placed his hands on her shoulders and held her as if he might never let go. "God was there for me when I needed Him, and you were like a steadfast pillar. But I turned away from both of you."

She smiled up at him. "That's in the past."

"I'll never turn from God again," he promised, "no more than I will ever turn away from you."

He dropped his hands down her arms and once again captured her hands in his.

"I love you, Ruthie. Will you take a chance on me? Will you marry me?"

She had always known God had chosen this man for her. And now, at long last, he'd proved it. "I've always been yours, Gray. You're the only man I've ever loved." Her spirit soared with so much happiness she could barely hold it all in. Her left hand clamped together in a prayer of thanksgiving. "Of course I'll marry you!"

Gray moved in to kiss her, then abruptly stopped. He lifted her left hand, his fingers shaping themselves around hers.

Thinking he found it silly, she started to shake her fingers loose, but he stopped her.

"I kind of like it," he said with a grin. "It *emu-ses* me. In fact—" he folded his own hand to match hers "—I might even start doing it myself. And there's no time like the present."

With that, he touched his fingertips to hers and made a smooching noise.

She laughed with delight, her voice seeming to echo in the empty sanctuary. Perhaps the echo was actually God, joining in their laughter.

And then Gray *really* kissed her.

* * * * *

Dear Reader,

One of my favorite memories of my grandmother is of her lining up all the grandchildren, telling each of us how smart, sweet and beautiful or handsome we were and sealing the declaration with a heartfelt hug and kiss. At one memorable family gathering, my twelve-year-old cousin had brought along a scruffy-looking friend who unexpectedly found himself in the receiving line with us. When Nanny got to the visitor, she didn't even pause at his dirty, ragamuffin appearance. Instead, she remarked on his lovely blue eyes, told him how precious he was, then hugged and kissed him just as she had the rest. The boy beamed under her doting attention, and that moment forever sealed in my heart the true meaning of family.

As one of six children in a yours-mine-and-ours union, I learned that families are more about love than they are about blood. More about commitment than bonds from birth. And in church I learned that, as children of God, we are all part of His holy family.

Later, drawn to the theme of family, especially of families by choice, I found myself fashioning Ruthie's "honorary grandparents" after my own big-hearted grandmother.

As for the hero? What red-blooded woman wouldn't want a caring, protective man like Gray to settle down with and start a family? A man devoted to those he loves. A family man.

From me and my family to you and yours…

Love and grace,

Carolyn Greene

Questions for Discussion:

1. As a teen, Ruthie's mother died, leaving her without family and with nowhere to go. Fortunately, she was taken in by a couple from church. Could you see yourself doing the same for a member of your community? What are the potential drawbacks? What unexpected blessings might you and they receive?

2. Gray's faith was shaken as the result of a traumatic experience in his life. Do you believe that when someone loses his faith, he also loses his salvation? What verse(s) in the Bible back up your belief?

3. If one partner's faith is weaker than the other's, does that mean they're "unequally yoked"? Why or why not?

4. If you knew of a Christian who had turned away from God, how would you handle the matter with them? Would you try to find ways to convince them of God's unshakeable love, or would you give that person distance to figure it out on his own?

5. Some people look at certain life events as random coincidences, and others see them as evidence of God working in their lives. How do you feel about that? What does the Bible say about it? What "coincidence" in your life do you believe was evidence of God in action?

6. Ruthie has an unusual way of praying. Where and how do you do most of your praying?

7. Ruthie's "honorary grandmother" was named Naoko. How is their relationship similar to, or different from, that of Ruth and Naomi in the Bible?

8. Sobo's doll was very important to her. How do you think she would have felt if it hadn't been found? Which of your possessions do you have the most sentimental attachment to, and why?

9. Like Gray, Mr. Denton was deeply affected by what he experienced during his military deployment. Do you think Ruthie should have done more (or less) to help him? Why or why not?

10. Ruthie and her roommates teamed up to form the group of stores called Abundance. In what ways have you teamed up with others to achieve something that was stronger than the sum of its parts?

11. A lot of water had passed under the bridge since Gray and Ruthie's breakup. Do you think broken couples can overcome their difficulties and eventually create an even stronger relationship than before? Why or why not?

COMING NEXT MONTH FROM
Love Inspired®

Available June 17, 2014

HER MONTANA COWBOY
Big Sky Centennial • by Valerie Hansen

When rodeo cowboy Ryan Travers comes to town, mayor's daughter Julie Shaw can't keep her eyes off him. Amid Jasper Gulch's centennial celebrations, they just may find true love!

THE BACHELOR NEXT DOOR
Castle Falls • by Kathryn Springer

Successful businessman Brendan Kane has made little room in his life for fun. Will his mother's hiring of Lily Michaels to renovate his family home bring him the laughter—and love—he's been missing?

REDEEMING THE RANCHER
Serendipity Sweethearts • by Deb Kastner

City boy Griff Haddon never thought he'd fall for the small town community of Serendipity—especially beautiful rancher Alexis Grainger. If he can forget his past hurts, this may just be his second chance at forever.

SMALL-TOWN HOMECOMING
Moonlight Cove • by Lissa Manley

Musician Curt Graham returns to Moonlight Cove to start a new life. Can beautiful innkeeper Jenna Flaherty see beyond his bad boy past and build a future together?

FOREVER A FAMILY
Rosewood, Texas • by Bonnie K. Winn

Widow Olivia Gray hopes volunteering at Rosewood's veterinary clinic will help her troubled son. But is veterinarian Zeke Harrison also the key to healing her broken heart?

THEIR UNEXPECTED LOVE
Second Time Around • by Kathleen Y'Barbo

Working together on a ministry project, Logan Burkett and spirited Pipa Gallagher clash from the beginning. Will they ever move past their differences and see that sometimes opposites really *do* attract?

LOOK FOR THESE AND OTHER LOVE INSPIRED BOOKS WHEREVER BOOKS ARE SOLD, INCLUDING MOST BOOKSTORES, SUPERMARKETS, DISCOUNT STORES AND DRUGSTORES.

LICNM0614

REQUEST YOUR FREE BOOKS!

2 FREE INSPIRATIONAL NOVELS
PLUS 2
FREE
MYSTERY GIFTS

Love Inspired

YES! Please send me 2 FREE Love Inspired® novels and my 2 FREE mystery gifts (gifts are worth about $10). After receiving them, if I don't wish to receive any more books, I can return the shipping statement marked "cancel." If I don't cancel, I will receive 6 brand-new novels every month and be billed just $4.74 per book in the U.S. or $5.24 per book in Canada. That's a saving of at least 21% off the cover price. It's quite a bargain! Shipping and handling is just 50¢ per book in the U.S. and 75¢ per book in Canada.* I understand that accepting the 2 free books and gifts places me under no obligation to buy anything. I can always return a shipment and cancel at any time. Even if I never buy another book, the two free books and gifts are mine to keep forever.

105/305 IDN F47Y

Name	(PLEASE PRINT)	
Address		Apt. #
City	State/Prov.	Zip/Postal Code
Signature (if under 18, a parent or guardian must sign)		

Mail to the Harlequin® Reader Service:
IN U.S.A.: P.O. Box 1867, Buffalo, NY 14240-1867
IN CANADA: P.O. Box 609, Fort Erie, Ontario L2A 5X3

**Are you a subscriber to Love Inspired books
and want to receive the larger-print edition?
Call 1-800-873-8635 or visit www.ReaderService.com.**

* Terms and prices subject to change without notice. Prices do not include applicable taxes. Sales tax applicable in N.Y. Canadian residents will be charged applicable taxes. Offer not valid in Quebec. This offer is limited to one order per household. Not valid for current subscribers to Love Inspired books. All orders subject to credit approval. Credit or debit balances in a customer's account(s) may be offset by any other outstanding balance owed by or to the customer. Please allow 4 to 6 weeks for delivery. Offer available while quantities last.

Your Privacy—The Harlequin® Reader Service is committed to protecting your privacy. Our Privacy Policy is available online at www.ReaderService.com or upon request from the Harlequin Reader Service.

We make a portion of our mailing list available to reputable third parties that offer products we believe may interest you. If you prefer that we not exchange your name with third parties, or if you wish to clarify or modify your communication preferences, please visit us at www.ReaderService.com/consumerchoice or write to us at Harlequin Reader Service Preference Service, P.O. Box 9062, Buffalo, NY 14269. Include your complete name and address.

LI13R

For the first time in longer than Ryan Travers could re-
call, he was having trouble keeping his mind on his work.
He couldn't have cared less about Jasper Gulch's missing
time capsule; it was pretty Julie Shaw who occupied his
thoughts.

"That's not good," he muttered as he stood on a metal
rung of the narrow bucking chute. This rangy pinto mare
wasn't called Widow-maker for nothing. He could not only
picture Julie Shaw as if she were standing right there next to
the chute gates, he could imagine her light, uplifting laughter.

Actually, he realized with a start, that *was* what he was
hearing. He started to glance over his shoulder, intending to
scan the nearby crowd and, hopefully, locate her.

"Clock's ticking, Travers," the chute boss grumbled.
"You gonna ride that horse or just look at her?"

Rather than answer with words, Ryan stepped across
the top of the chute, raised his free hand over his head and
leaned way back. Then he nodded to the gateman.

The latch clicked.

The mare leaped.

Ryan didn't attempt to do anything but ride until he heard
the horn blast announcing his success. Then he straightened

as best he could and worked his fingers loose with his free hand while pickup men maneuvered close enough to help him dismount.

To Ryan's delight, Julie Shaw and a few others he recognized from before were watching. They had parked a flatbed farm truck near the fence beside the grandstand and were watching from secure perches in its bed.

Julie had both arms raised and was still cheering so wildly she almost knocked her hat off. "Woo-hoo! Good ride, cowboy!"

Ryan's "Thanks" was swallowed up in the overall din from the rodeo fans. Clearly, Julie wasn't the only spectator who had been favorably impressed.

He knew he should immediately report to the area behind the strip chutes and pick up his rigging. And he would. In a few minutes. As soon as he'd spoken to his newest fan.

Don't miss the romance between Julie and rodeo hero Ryan in HER MONTANA COWBOY by Valerie Hansen, available July 2014 from Love Inspired®.

LIEXP0614R

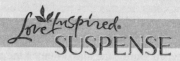
When a widow is stalked and taunted by memories from her tragic past, can the man who rescued her years ago come to her aid again?

Read on for a preview of PROTECTIVE INSTINCTS by Shirlee McCoy, the first book in her brand-new MISSION: RESCUE series.

"Who would want to hurt you, Raina?" Jackson asked her.

"No one," she replied, her mind working frantically, going through faces and names and situations.

"And yet, someone chased you through the woods. That same person nearly ran me down. Doesn't sound like someone who feels all warm and fuzzy when he thinks of you."

"Maybe he was a vagrant, and I scared him."

"Maybe." He didn't sound like he believed it, and she wasn't sure she did, either.

She'd heard something that had woken her from the nightmare.

A child crying? Her neighbor Larry wandering around? An intruder trying to get into the house?

The last thought made her shudder, and she pulled her coat a little closer. "I think I'd know it if someone had a bone to pick with me."

"That's usually the case, but not always. Could be you upset a coworker, said no to a guy who wanted you to say yes—"

She snorted at that, and Jackson frowned. "You've been a widow for four years. It's not that far-fetched an idea."

"If you got a good look at my social life you wouldn't be saying that."

Samuel yawned loudly and slid down on the pew, his arms crossed over his chest, his eyelids drooping. The ten-year-old looked cold and tired, and she wanted to get him home and tuck him into bed.

"I'll go talk to Officer Wallace," Jackson responded. "See if he's ready to let us leave."

"He's going to have to be. Samuel—"

A door slammed, the sound so startling Raina jumped.

She grabbed Samuel's shoulder, pulled him into the shelter of her arms.

"Is someone else in the church?" Jackson demanded, his gaze on the door that led from the sanctuary into the office wing.

"There shouldn't be."

"Stay put. I'm going to check things out."

He strode away, and she wanted to call out and tell him to be careful.

She pressed her lips together, held in the words she knew she didn't need to say. She'd seen him in action, knew just how smart and careful he was.

Jackson could take care of himself.

*Will Jackson discover the stalker and help
Raina find a second chance at love?*

*Pick up PROTECTIVE INSTINCTS to find out.
Available July 2014 wherever
Love Inspired® Suspense books are sold.*

Love Inspired®

THE BACHELOR NEXT DOOR

by

Kathryn Springer

Dedicating all his time to the family business isn't easy for Brendan Kane. But he owes his foster parents big-time for taking him and his brothers in. And if he has to give up the possibility of a relationship—so be it. So when Brendan's mother hires Lily Michaels to redecorate the family home, it doesn't matter to Brendan that Lily is beautiful. And funny. And smart. He has no time for distractions. Can Lily show him there's more to life…and that it includes a future together?

Castle Falls

Three rugged brothers meet their matches.

Available July 2014 wherever
Love Inspired books and ebooks are sold.

LI87896